Hook, Line and Single

Hook, Line and Single

MARCIA KING-GAMBLE

sepia™

HOOK, LINE AND SINGLE

ISBN-13: 978-0-373-83118-0
ISBN-10:   0-373-83118-8

www.kimanipress.com

Printed in U.S.A.

"To the single ladies still looking for that perfect fit. Beware of Reeds in sheep's clothing. Give your heart carefully!"

CHAPTER 1

It's a dog-eat-dog world out there. If you can't run with the pack, you're left behind sniffing dirt.

I got left behind once and I don't plan on that ever happening again. Now I'm on a mission to find Mr. Right. I've determined that tonight could very well be the night.

My name is Roxanne Ingram. People call me Roxi for short. I'm African American, thirty-nine years old—a sneeze away from forty—and I'm a business owner. I think I'm a pretty good package but I'm beginning to question whether others see me as such. Like right now I'm asking myself what I'm doing in Manhattan at a speed-dating event.

Blame it on Margot Nanton, who is my best friend and who talked me into going to the Roosevelt Hotel. And now here I am mingling and smiling so wide you can practically see my cavities. And I'm making the rounds, in boots that are pinching, scoping out possibilities and hoping to find Lord knows what. Aaah! I want to go home.

I pat my straightened hair with the burgundy streaks that's pinned up into one of those swirly dos. Meanwhile two women are yakking in my ear and I haven't a clue what they're saying. This Long Island woman hasn't quite gotten the hang of Ebonics, and the roly-poly hip-hop girl and the J Lo wannabe are really going at it. Getting down.

"You need ta chill," roly-poly says to J Lo.

"No, I need ta be hooked up with one ah dem fine brothas." The hip-hop girl twirled one of her many earrings and looked around, she locked eyes with a dark-skinned man with a shaved head and gold chains matching his teeth.

"Ya want ta get laid, it's as easy as this." Roly-poly pops her fingers and begins inching her way in the direction of the man they've targeted. "Now hear me conversate."

A coordinator rings a bell and shoos us into an adjoining room. Aaaah! I want to go home.

Margot and I have fake names. I am Scarlet and Margot is Yolanda. We probably sound like two exotic dancers but Margot couldn't think of anything else at the time. I'm here because I'm getting over getting dumped and I need to start putting a big toe back in the water.

Margot and I sit two tables apart. We are separated

by Teresa and Wendy. Teresa is a plump Puerto Rican stuffed into a dress that is way too tight. Rolls of flesh pop over the top and sides. She reminds me of a child's toy, the kind that bobs, bobbles and never topples over.

Wendy is an African-American woman with one of those hairstyles that looks like a fountain. She occupies the seat next to Margot. I am fascinated by the cascades of hair in different shades of pink. I am fascinated by her pierced nose and the hoop in her bottom lip. I don't even want to think what other parts of her anatomy has rings.

I pick up the sheet of paper with the instructions. We have six minutes to exchange life stories and make an impression. When the bell rings the man moves on to the next woman. There's a one-minute period to check "yes" or strike him out of your life forever.

Margot and I shoot each other amused looks. This is woman power. The hostess rings her bell.

"Welcome! I'm Judi. I'm your coordinator," she chimes in one of those squeaky voices that sounds as if she inhaled a mouthful of helium. "We're here to have fun, right? Just let me go over a couple of minor housekeeping details with you then we'll get started."

Judi begins ticking off the dos and don'ts of speed dating on her fingers.

"Be respectful in terms of the questions you ask. You're here to meet Mr. Right, right? Keep things light, positive and upbeat. You don't want to scare off any would-be honeys. After I count to ten we'll start. One, two, three…"

While she is counting I check out the male prospects—all in my opinion a scary lot. I already know I will have little in common with them. I remind myself I'm here to get over Dave, my latest disappointment.

Dave and I were dating for several months. Things were going well, or so I thought, then one day out of the blue he called and told me it was over. Being dumped is one thing but when you learn you're being replaced by a man that's an entirely different matter.

I will not think about Dave or how ugly I'd gotten. I'd been at my worst and it wasn't pretty. After a suitable amount of time I'd brushed myself off and made myself get back out there again. This time I'm the one who intends to play the field. I'll be keeping my options open.

I haven't seen any buttoned-down men here, just lots of open-necked shirts with chest hair protruding and lots of flashy jewelry. You know the kind. Big thick chains and manacles circling the wrist. I like my men looking like men: well groomed and conservative.

But there is one smooth dark-skinned man with glasses that captures my interest. He is dressed in a tailored suit and understated paisley tie. He seems out of place in this sea of urban characters as if he's not sure what he is doing here.

Another man, still wearing his winter coat, has potential. Clothing hides a lot but he seems to be in decent shape. An expensive-looking cashmere sweater peeks out from under the open coat. His teeth sparkle, white on white, a nice contrast to his Hershey-colored skin.

"Ten," the hostess finishes.

We are off.

Bachelor number one sticks out a hand before sitting down. It is limp when I shake it.

"Michael Winthrop, Scarlet." His eyes are fastened on the name badge above my left breast or maybe it's my breast that's got him spellbound. I don't want to think about it. "You've got beautiful cinnamon skin," he says.

I thank him and flash him a perfect set of whites. Heck, I paid enough for them.

Michael is an overweight kid, probably in his mid to late twenties. He has one of those great big smiles that wreathes his face in triple chins. He sounds very eager to make me like him.

"What do you do, Michael?"

The sales pitch follows. He tells me he's a marketing executive for a Madison Avenue firm. He wants to know if I enjoy trips to the Caribbean since he spends two weeks of the winter at Sam Lord's Castle; a luxury hotel. He wants to know how I feel about children. He has a two-year-old from a previous marriage.

The alarm bells go off. I get the feeling Michael might be shopping for a housekeeper and nanny to help out. He isn't a bad guy, just not for me. At thirty-nine I'm not looking for anyone quite as young. I've raised my child, Lindsay, and a two-year-old is not part of the plan. I am very happy when the bell rings and he has to move on.

Bachelor number two, Colby, slides into the seat and begins drumming his fingers on the oak table. He must be nervous because his deodorant is failing him. He's got ring around the armpits and the sweet-sour odor coming from him makes me want to gag. I try putting him at ease by asking the questions, but all of my inquiries meet with one-word answers. Next.

I check "no" on my card and hope Colby's stink doesn't linger. Wendy, the woman next to me, is in for a treat.

Bachelor number three is unremarkably boring and

is a blur. I don't recall a single thing he says. Bachelor number four leaves a lot to be desired in the grammar department. He says he's a professional but I can't imagine what company would hire him. Then again corporate isn't what it used to be.

In between bell rings, I am trying to catch Margot's eye and tip her off as to what to expect. We know each other so well that a raised eyebrow and a fluttered eyelash speak volumes. We try this silent communication before the next bachelor sits down.

I've about given up on the crowd when bachelor number eight takes a seat. He doesn't seem the type to attend a speed-dating event. This guy is reserved and classy. His cognac complexion glows. He is tall, athletic and clean shaven. His hair is trimmed very close to the scalp and he looks like he could be a Brooks Brothers ad. He is my kind of man.

"I'm Scarlet," I say, flashing my big smile.

He nods his head. "Leo." He gives the hand I offer a firm grip.

Leo puts on his glasses and takes out a set of index cards from the breast pocket of a navy jacket. I presume there are questions written on them. He lays them on the table in front of him.

Too anal for me. But I'm intrigued. He's an African-American male of a certain age and appears to be the full package: fine, in shape, successful. That's as good as it gets. No baby-mama drama so far. Why not hear him out.

Leo's jacket comes off to reveal a monogrammed shirt, mother-of-pearl cuff links at the cuffs. Sweet. He sweeps an index card up in hands that have seen a manicurist and looks at me.

"Nice hair," he says, and then focuses on the card in front of him. "If you and I were on a date at a restaurant and one of my old girlfriends comes over. How would you handle it?"

I hike an eyebrow and parry back. "If she's an old girlfriend why would it matter?"

"Good answer." Leo's sherry-colored eyes twinkle behind his glasses. I feel as if I'm on a game show. I can't wait to see what else is next. "You're a secure and confident woman," he adds.

"That may be the case but why would I get bent out of shape if she's an old girlfriend. I'm not insecure."

Leo peers at me over those attractive horn-rimmed spectacles. "Women who come to these things usually have self-esteem problems."

"Not this one? And what about you men? Why are you here?"

Leo stares at his manicured nails. "I'm here to see what's out there."

I smile sweetly. "So am I. Does that mean you and I have something in common?"

"You're more together than most," Leo has the gall to say.

"You must be meeting the wrong women."

The bell rings and it is over.

He flips a business card at me and then gives me that obnoxious finger. You know the one, a synchronicity of thumb and index finger, as if he's pointing a gun. He moves onto Wendy.

I am down to bachelor number eleven. I am chastising myself for letting Margot talk me into this when John sits down. He is ex-military with a brush cut and the manners that goes along with years of discipline.

"Evening, ma'am, I'm John."

Ma'am? God, I feel old. My smile wavers but I manage, "Evening, John, I'm Scarlet."

"As in O'Hara?'

We both crack up. Under that stiff exterior lies a droll sense of humor. John gets it and possibly gets me.

"Ladies first," he says, giving me a chance to ask questions.

I go for the standard. "What do you do?"

"Take a guess."

"You're an attorney?" He has that poised look to him.

"No."

"Pastor?"

I am fishing, no pastor I know looks like him, but there are always surprises.

"Agent," John says when I've pretty much exhausted all of my options.

"What kind of agent?"

"Sports agent. I represent some of the biggest names in the business."

John reels off a bunch of names that are supposed to impress me. When my eyes glaze over he takes pity.

"You don't follow basketball, do you?"

"I don't follow sports, period."

"What do you follow?"

"My heart."

The devil made me do it. I swear.

"And what is your heart telling you to do now?" John asks.

"Put on my track shoes and run."

John waggles a finger at me. "Now, that's not very nice."

"I'm not nice."

"I want your phone number,"

He shoves his business card in my hand and, palm open, waits for mine.

I rifle through my purse, find my card, the one that says Owner and CEO of Wife for Hire. I slide it over.

John glances at it and stares at me. "Impressive. You're an independent woman."

The last bachelor; a lanky white guy sits down. He gawks at me.

"Is there something the matter?" I ask. Someone needed to start the conversation.

"Wr-wr-ong? Everything's r-r-right. You're beau-beautiful. You...you're tall and elegant, j-just like I...I...I like."

His name badge reads, Neal.

Neal sounds sincere but I'm not interested. It has nothing to do with his stutter. He just isn't my type. I thank him and hope the bell rings soon. It's the longest six minutes of my life.

Sure, I've been told I'm beautiful. Men will tell you pretty much anything. After a while you don't just believe them. The right outfit and makeup do wonders for a woman, and tonight I look good. I'm wearing boots with heels and a wraparound dress made famous by the designer Diane Von Furstenberg. I've had no time to flat-iron or curl my hair, so on went the mousse before I pinned it up.

Margot, my friend, on the other hand, is beautiful. She is fragile and petite and men want to take care of her. She is wearing cropped black wool pants that skim the ankles and a turquoise off-the-shoulder top, and she looks like a Barbie doll.

"H-have you ever d-d-dated outside of your race before?" Neal asks, looking as if any answer I give might very well destroy him.

I give him my wide-eyed stare. "Why?"

"Be-because I w-want to know how you would feel about going out with me?"

I tap the card in front of me. "That's what these are for, Neal. If we both check 'yes,' we're a match. If not…" I shrug.

"I'd r-r-rather know now."

"Look, Neal, you and I don't know each other. You're not even asking questions. We don't know if we're compatible. I've got six kids. All with different fathers. My mother lives with me. I'm looking for someone to take me, the kids and mom out of Queens. Can you do that?"

Neal looks slightly dazed. "Y-y-you're pulling my l-l-l-leg, r-r-right?"

"I'm dead serious." I don't even smile.

The bell jingles, thank God. The evening is over and I am done. I am off my stool in an instant and on my way over to get Margot. Neal is still sitting in shock.

We hand the coordinator our completed cards then

walk three blocks to the Indian restaurant on the corner. I need a drink badly.

Over samosas, tandoori chicken and a veggie dish, we compare notes.

"I'm hoping Leo and Kyle call me," Margot says.

"You're joking, right?" Leo is the man who is full of himself. Kyle is an investment-banker type. Neither has impressed me much, but Margot and I have different tastes in men. Always have and always will. Scary.

I know why Margot has picked both men. She thinks they can give her what she wants. Margot is about material things and can be quite superficial.

I begin to question whether I am seeking the impossible. I own a business. I have a house. I have a child in college. My life is full.

Yet here I am trying out a brave new world of speed dating, chat rooms and cybersex. I must be losing my mind.

CHAPTER 2

I go to bed that night thinking I'm in way over my head. Who needs to get out there at this age when you don't need a man to survive? I'm from good old hardy Caribbean stock. I'm neither clingy nor dependent. I'm what you call a happy divorcée, and I'm not looking to get married soon. Been there. Done that. Not sure I want to go there again.

I've been told that most women who've been married feel like me and we remain hopeful that one day *Mr. Right* will come along. So we keep searching for that elusive one.

The phone rings when I've run out of sheep to count. I can't imagine who would be calling after midnight. Then I remember it's still early on the West Coast. It could be Dave, the shithead who broke things off. But I doubt it.

I grab the receiver anyway and deepen my voice. "Hello."

"Roxanne is that you?"

No one calls me Roxanne except that lug.

"Yeah, it's me. My number hasn't changed."

I hold my breath and wait. We used to have an open-ended arrangement; a no-strings attached policy. All I'd ever asked of Dave was his honesty. Honesty he didn't or couldn't do well.

"I want to see you, Roxi," Dave says.

"What happened to that man you fell in love with?"

"I had to let him go."

I am wide-awake now, my heart palpitating, but not in anticipation of him telling me he wants me back. I squeeze the receiver imagining it's his neck. Pop! Pop! And I exhale. I know my blood pressure must be close to stroke level.

"You dumped me," I accuse. "What makes you think I want to see you?"

"Ahh, doll, don't be like that. We had fun together. We can still have fun."

It would be a cold day in hell when I let that happen. I choke back a colorful expletive, stab the button on the portable phone and cut him off midjabber.

So much for that!

Now I think back, David James, dark as night with velvet-soft skin and a voice that made me shiver, had always been sneaky and self-focused. It was all about Dave. Any fool would have seen it coming.

It's a painful lesson to learn, ladies. Guard your

heart against men you can't pin down. If it smells like a rat and acts like a rat, usually it's a big fat rat. Go with your intuition. Trust your gut. A rodent can't change his claws just as the leopard can't change his spots.

I plump up my pillow, position it under my head, and give good old sleep a college try. Eventually I must have dozed, because the next thing I know my alarm is going off, and I am in that numb state when you're not sure whether it's day or night. I have to check to be sure. I have a business to run and can't afford to laze around.

Wife for Hire, the company I own, pays the bills. I'd spent eight years in human resources and experienced the corporate world firsthand. It stinks. So one day I up and fire my boss. I use the savings from my 401(k) to set up my own company, figuring there are people like me out there who don't have the time to clean a house or pay a bill. They need Wife for Hire and will willingly pay.

Over time I slowly build up a reputation. Today I am at the point where I don't owe a thing. My salary takes care of my mortgage and my daughter, Lindsay's, college tuition.

Wife for Hire is a full-service outfit. We charge plenty for our service but we do a better job than the competition. We do everything from personal shopping to renewing driver's licenses. My team even helped one bachelor bury his mother.

I shower, gulp coffee and boot up my computer. After wading through business e-mails, I return a few calls and get into a screaming match with the bank because they've screwed up a deposit. I am about to check on my employees, Kazoo, Lydia and Vance, all part-timers, when my cell phone jingles.

Caller ID comes in useful for screening out people you don't want to hear from. It's Margot, probably wanting to rehash last evening's events. Guilty for considering not picking up, I force exuberance into my voice.

"Hey, girl, what's up?"

Sniffles on the other end. Not a good sign. But I should get used to this drama.

I met Margot Nanton at the gym when I was newly divorced and badly needed a friend. She was fresh out of a divorce herself, and not at all happy about it. In fact, she still isn't. As we peddled our bikes side by side, we began talking about the difficulties of being single, and we began comparing notes about lame dates and poor sexual performance. Over time, a strong friendship developed.

"You'll never guess what that bastard's done now."

Margot wails in one of her trademark run-on sentences.

That bastard usually means her ex-husband, Earl.

"What's Earl done?" I ask dutifully, preparing myself for at least a ten-minute dissertation on what a jerk her ex is.

"Bounced my alimony check. Now what am I supposed to do? I have bills to pay."

"Oh, my." I roll my eyes. Not that I'm not sympathetic, but this is getting old. Margot needs to move on. She refuses to find a job, and that fat alimony check is her only source of income. She's told me she has no intention of remarrying, ever, and giving up that salary.

I listen with one ear and wisely keep silent. I have my own troubles. Margot is going on now about how Earl owes her. I've heard this story a thousand times, about how he talked her into quitting her teaching job when they first got married. How she became his personal slave, cooking his meals, ironing his shirts and giving birth to two children that had been taken away from her when she'd had her nervous breakdown. He owes her plenty for having an affair with his assistant—a series of assistants as it turns out.

I am tempted to say, "There aren't any victims in love, hon. Just volunteers," but I keep my mouth shut.

If I say that to her she'll go ballistic.

"So what am I going to do?" Margot wails again. "How am I going to pay the mortgage?"

Better not remind her that she has more than adequate savings put aside. Monies she's been stashing away from the days when Earl took care of everything. She showed me her portfolio once. The woman has enough to buy two houses, cash.

"What you always do," I say patiently. "Wait Earl out. He'll send you another check."

"Jackson will take care of him," she sniffs.

Jackson was her attorney.

Despite all her bitching, Margot still loves Earl. She will use any excuse to contact him, albeit through her attorney. I'm not sure Earl is exactly immune to her, either.

Margot has issues all because of a troubled childhood growing up in a household with no father figure. There'd been one string of uncles after another coming through that house. Some of those uncles had molested her.

I forgive her a lot and ignore the ricocheting moods. She is like a yo-yo hitting a high one minute and rock bottom the next. The medication she is taking is supposed to keep her stable. In my humble opinion the most recent prescription isn't working.

"What if I show up at Earl's condo and confront him and his latest?" she moans.

"Not a good idea. You'll be violating your restraining order and you'll get arrested," I answer dryly.

Earl had been forced to request a "no contact" order after Margot broke in and tore up his place. She'd driven by one day and seen a sporty Volkswagen convertible Beetle out front. The kind the twentysomething crowd likes. She'd ended up with a fistful of the assistant's hair in her hand and did some serious damage to Earl's watchamacallit.

"Guess what? Dave called me," I say, hoping to take Margot's mind off her own worries.

"Bastard!

It is Margot's favorite word. "Betcha anything he got dumped. You don't need some guy on the down low."

I think the same but don't need to hear it. Today is another day and I am still giving Internet dating a try, which means there are more where he came from. I refuse to go down the horrible road of depression and recrimination. I truly believe if you fall off a horse you get back on and ride. And if push comes to shove I have Max Porter; charming and irresponsible. He takes care of my physical needs and then some. The problem is Max isn't around that often.

When I finally hang up I decide to go in search of the stray cat that lives in my backyard shed. I've been feeding Bo Jangles for over two years and I haven't seen him for almost a week now. I hope nothing terrible happened. Maybe another family is feeding him and so he abandoned me.

I wander down the block, stopping to exchange a word or two with the mostly-stay-at-home moms and the retirees living on my street. The town I live in, Malverne, is a quaint little hamlet not far from New York City. It's a throwback to the sixties and people still say hello. Homes are nestled on quaint tree-lined streets and there's a town center with a restaurant, bakery, newsstand and bar.

I rustle the hedges and call, "Here, kitty, kitty. Bo Jangles, where are you?" Puffs of smoke curl from my mouth. It isn't officially winter yet but it sure is getting here fast.

"Are you looking for your cat? Mrs. Ingram?" Jessica, the terror of the neighborhood, asks.

"Bo Jangles isn't my cat," I explain. "He's a stray. He's a big old marmalade-colored cat with one eye missing. Have you seen him?"

Jessica's eyes widen. "No. But if I do see him I'll bring him to your house."

I thank her, knowing it would never happen. Bo

Jangles isn't about to let a stranger get close to him. Even after two years we still maintain a respectful distance from each other.

One hour later, all I've succeeded in doing is tiring myself out and looking disheveled. I trudge back to the house, work on payroll and pay my bills online. After that I check my personal e-mail to see if anyone new has surfaced on the dating site.

Internet dating is something I've come to kicking and screaming. If you're a busy person, finding a mate the conventional way just isn't going to happen. The good ones are usually married or gay.

After mourning my dear departed husband a suitable time, I put myself back into circulation. And, no, I'm not a widow, my ex left one day to find himself and never came back. He claimed the responsibility of a wife and child was too much for him. During this search for self he managed to hook up with a woman who needs him. And he doesn't seem to mind her three children.

Margot is the one who'd convinced me to get back into the game. She'd browbeaten me and suggested Internet dating, calling it not only anonymous, but an endless candyland of men. It's a numbers game, and if you hang in there long enough, there's bound to be a custom fit, she said.

I come from the days of the classified ads so this isn't entirely foreign. Just new technology to master, and coded messages to decipher. And here I am, six months later, practically a pro, toggling between three dating sites and getting more and more disillusioned by the canned profiles that say nothing.

"You're working the odds," Margot always reminded me when I wailed about what my life had come to. "The more darts you throw at a board, the more likely one will hit the mark."

She is one to talk; though she's working at it, she still hasn't found Earl's replacement.

I hear a plaintive meow coming from the vicinity of my backyard. Bo Jangles. The main man in my life has come home.

I leave the computer on and bolt for the back door. My adopted cat, looking bedraggled and road weary, as if he's been in dozens of fights, is standing in front of the shed that is his home; even his good eye is drooping.

"Bo Jangles." I hold my arms wide. "Where have you been?"

A hungry meow greets me.

I go back inside and get a can of cat food from the cupboard. I plop it in his bowl, and set it down on the steps of the patio. Then I go back inside and wait, pressing my nose against the glass pane to see what he will do.

Not three minutes after I've retreated, Bo Jangles limps toward the step and makes short work of his food.

I feel lighter now as if a huge burden has been lifted. My attention turns back to the e-mails and profiles I've abandoned. I have to be a masochist to do this, I chide, expose my heart to the walking wounded, the unable, the unwilling and the more-than-a-tad-bit confused. In the cyberworld hearts are disposable and *love* makes you an easy hit. *Fun* means willing to have sex.

I return to the profile and photo of someone who's new. I am now a pro at deciphering truth from fiction. *Six feet tall* usually means *five foot seven with lifts. A few extra pounds* means *fat,* and *professional* can mean anything from *stock clerk* to *dog trainer,* take your pick.

This latest calls himself Big Jim. Go figure whether he is describing his weight, height or equipment. I strongly suspect it's the last. He says he's in real estate. And he's written me a reasonably amusing e-mail with no misspellings. That in and of itself is a big plus.

I shoot back a quick answer and return to reading my mail. The next guy calls himself Flyboy. He and I have been trying to get together for weeks but our schedules aren't coinciding. Plus, he's canceled on me last minute one too many times. I hit the delete button and zap him into cyberspace.

The next e-mail is from a man whose screen name I recognize. Ted is from Alaska and is a military type. By location alone he should be GU—geographically undesirable—but I am willing to give him a try. He and I click on a lot of different levels and I use him as a sounding board.

I shoot off more e-mails, dissect a profile or two and decide I need to focus on the job that keeps a roof over my head and food in my mouth.

I read more e-mails but this time they are all business related.

One client needs me to buy a wedding gift for his boss. I don't consider that urgent since the wedding is weeks away. Another wants a masseuse to come to her home, so I make an appointment and set it up for tomorrow. Businessmen, probably my best customers, need their bills paid. I put that at the top of the list.

And as usual there is an assortment of mundane requests: pets to be fed, plants watered and vehicles needing servicing. The more tedious chores I farm out to my student part-timers.

Just as I am finishing up, the phone rings. I glance

at the caller ID and grab the receiver. It is Lindsay, my college-age daughter.

I adore that child, though she is an expert at trying my patience. Even so, we are more like sisters than mother and daughter.

I immediately go into "mom mode."

"Hey, baby. Watcha doing?" I coo.

"Studying, Mom, always studying. I need a favor,"

I square my shoulders and wait for the request. The bank of Roxanne Ingram is always open.

CHAPTER 3

"I need money," my daughter whines.

What's new? I roll my eyes. Lindsay always needs money.

But the sound of her voice makes my lips curve into a smile. It always does. I live for this child. It's been me and Lindsay against the world for a long, long time. We've taken care of each other through the bitterness of a divorce. We've survived, thrived and managed to become best friends.

"How much this time?" I ask.

"Five hundred bucks."

"Five hundred bucks! That's a lot of money. What's going on, Lindsay? Be straight with me."

My nineteen-year-old rambles on about a ski trip her friends are taking. They are planning on flying to Jackson Hole, Wyoming. As far as I am concerned the outing doesn't constitute an emergency, but to someone Lindsay's age missing out is a major calamity.

Ever since her father left us, I've tried my best to give that child everything she wants. But a ski trip sounds frivolous and a little decadent. I was almost thirty years old before I went skiing, and most of the time I spent on my back.

"Please, Mom," she cajoles.

That child knows how to play me. She knows that plaintive whine will get her anything she wants.

"Okay, I'll put up half if you find the other half," I say, relenting. "Ask your dad for a contribution."

"I already did. All he says is black kids don't need ski trips."

She is right. Kane can be a real ass at times. Successful as he is, he still carries around an oversize chip on his shoulder. Kane is a mortgage banker.

"How badly do you want to go?" I counter, and prepare to hear the litany that is sure to follow.

For fifteen minutes I listen to how difficult being a college student is, and hasn't she made the dean's list every semester?

That guilting gets her another fifty bucks.

"Okay, I'm done. Better call your father."

No sooner have I hung up, the calendar on my computer beeps, alerting me to an appointment. Mr. X, my client is hot. His international flight is scheduled to land in an hour, and I've promised to pick him up at JFK airport. The man is out of the country more often than he is in, but his business is regular and he pays me well.

At first I used to send limousines to pick him up, but one evening he flew in unexpectedly from Rome and called me, desperate. No taxi for him. I couldn't find a limousine on such short notice so off to the airport I went. I won't leave a customer stranded.

Mr. X was waiting outside the customs area with a large Gucci garment bag draped over one arm. A Smarte Carte piled high with matching luggage surrounded him. And as usual he was hidden behind expensive dark glasses.

After I'd gotten him settled in the Land Rover, he flashed those pearly whites at me and handed me a box of Bacci.

"This is for you," he said in that continental accent of his.

Feeling as if he'd just handed me the winning lottery ticket, I drove him into The City and dropped him off at his brownstone in the tony silk-stocking district of Manhattan.

I was being paid triple my going rate for being so responsive on such short notice. After that little episode, X always requested that I picked him up personally. Only a fool would say no. I can't afford to turn down that kind of money. Besides, I am curious about him and he makes my insides quiver. There is something about a black man who flies all over the globe,

speaks with an accent and pays his bills with a corporate platinum American Express card that gets your attention.

I don't know what X does for a living but I do know
he has some bucks. And I do know that I am spending
more and more of my waking hours fantasizing about
him. Full-blown, X-rated fantasies, mind you. The
kind that make a woman wet.

Sometimes I will picture myself lying under X's hard
nut-brown body, his long, tapered fingers stroking my
back. I've envisioned those eyes behind the shielding
sunglasses, burning into me. And if I concentrate really
hard I can feel X sliding in and out of me, whispering
words that are meant for my ears only. I know he
speaks a number of foreign languages. I have heard
him on the phone.

Sometimes he goes to it in a rush of Italian. At times
he converses in Spanish, at other times French and there
are others he speaks that, frankly, I don't have a clue.

Just thinking about Mr. X is making me orgasmic.
Hell, who needs Dave or some battery-operated device
when I have X? One "bella," in my ear and the whole
world literally stops.

I've been told every woman needs a fantasy lover,
and that failing, a back-up man, or should that be the
plan? You should have a man who worships you, and

another who knows exactly how to hit your G-spot. If they can both keep an erection even better, and if their mouths and fingers are synchronized, you've died and gone to pig heaven.

Is it so absurd to think I can get everything I want? No harm in trying. The Internet helps you meet people that you never in your wildest dreams ever would meet.

I am going to be late. Not a good thing. I pride myself on being reliable and dependable. These are all qualities that make Wife for Hire stand out from the rest.

Hopping into the Land Rover, I stomp on that accelerator and take off. I make good time until I get to Queens. The Belt Parkway has bumper-to-bumper traffic and by the time I inch my way to the airport entrance, I am spitting and snarling. It must be some nasty accident ahead.

"Dammit!" I yell, thumping the steering wheel and cussing up a storm. I reach into my purse, find my cell phone, clamp on earphones and punch in X's programmed number. Voice mail pops on. That means one of three things: X has turned off his cell phone; the flight from Milan is delayed; or if I am lucky he is working his way through customs. Number two and three sound like good options to me.

Earphones still on, I punch the number again just to listen to X's seductive message.

"Prego. You've reached 212 555-3145. At the sound of the beep you know what to do. Ciao."

I know what I want to do, all right. I want to jump his bones and put common sense on the back burner just for one night. How shameless I am.

The blast of car horns brings me back to the ugly reality of where I am, sitting in airport traffic. Irritated motorists are screaming obscenities at each other. My fantasies are over. I inch along until I see the signs for the terminals ahead.

Traffic comes to a dead halt again. In moments I am back to indulging in erotic musings. Mr. X is in the passenger seat next to me, one copper-colored arm draped around my shoulders, the other stroking my thigh.

Heat is radiating from his palms as his nimble fingers stroke the flesh on my legs. A couple of featherlike touches cause my stomach to flutter and my heartbeat to accelerate. I am pulsating and moist, wishing I can push my Victoria's Secret thong aside, open his fly and have him inside.

Behind me a driver sits on his horn. His foul expletives rip loose over the noise. New York is reality. Time here waits for no man. Impatience rules.

"Stupid women drivers!" someone calls. I am hoping they're not referring to me.

Another motorist attempts to come around me. He almost collides with a minivan with the same idea.

"Eat dirt and die, cretin!" I shout.

Since traffic is now moving, I step on the accelerator and shoot ahead.

The digital clock on my dashboard confirms I am over twenty minutes late. But my cell phone hasn't yet rung. Traffic slows again. A silver Toyota the size of a pretzel is being hauled off by a tow truck. The drivers involved in the accident are on the side of the road, screaming and duking it out, while two of New York's finest try to put an end to the fight.

The driver ahead of me slows down and continues to gawk.

"Enough, already," I grumble, resigned to being even later than I already am.

Another twenty minutes goes by before I slide into a parking spot across from Delta's terminal. Keys in hand, I race toward the baggage area. By some miracle my cell phone still hasn't rung.

Mr. X is waiting curbside, hidden behind his usual dark glasses. His hands rests on the handle of a cart piled high with baggage.

"I'm sorry," I huff. "There was an accident. I tried calling you."

X lays a gloved hand on my shoulder. I am out of breath and not just from the running.

"You worry too much, bella. I have been waiting maybe five minutes."

I have fantasies about that hand. I smile up into those shrouded eyes, wondering how a man who has traveled all the way from Milan, manages to look so rested and relaxed. His silver-flecked curls are meticulously trimmed, not a hair put of place. His tailored gray slacks that still hold their crease peek from under a Burberry coat. There is just the faintest smell of ginger spice to him.

I am Bella. Beautiful. My professionalism kicks in. Maybe he calls every woman Bella?

I shoot him a rueful grin. "I can bring the car around if you'd like," I say. "The cops are a bear about double parking."

I need to put space between us and collect myself.

"I will walk with you," he says. One leather-gloved palm taps the handle of the Smarte Carte holding his luggage. "This will make it easy. Besides, I need the exercise. I have been seated far too long." He bends his wrist revealing what looks to be a Baume and Mercier watch. "Already eleven hours. Far too long."

Mr. X has been my client for going on two years now. This is the most we've ever said to each other.

I reach across to take possession of his cart. I am his chauffeur after all.

"Bella, please, I insist."

He's called me "bella" again, and my insides are quivering.

X holds steadfast to the trolley and effortlessly pulls it behind him. He inhales audibly. The autumn air is crisp. Invigorating.

"Feels good to be back," he says, holding out his free hand to me. Hand in hand we walk across the street.

This new shyness I've developed comes and goes. It reminds me of a first date I had with Vernon, a doctor I'd met on the dating site. It took me three weeks to answer his message and all because of the photo he'd posted.

I'm not a shallow person. What I am is visual. If I can't picture myself sleeping with a man then I won't accept a second date. And I couldn't picture myself sitting across from Vernon much less getting next to him.

Vernon's photo on the site was what my grandmother used to call boo-boo ugly. Nevertheless I agreed to meet him in person and to my surprise he was hot. The electric sparks shooting off us could ignite a room.

But Vernon also came with three kids and a wife that was supposedly an ex but was not. Vernon and the Mrs. couldn't live together but couldn't live apart. The kids ruled. He used them to conduct negotiations between us. If Vernon was busy, which was almost always, the kids called on his behalf. Needless to say Vernon and I didn't last long.

X clears his throat. We are standing in front of the Land Rover and I'm not sure how long we've been there. Embarrassed, I click open the back hatch and reach for his luggage. But he deftly tosses the pieces inside and climbs into the passenger seat.

In minutes he is asleep or at least appears so. I fantasize, while navigating what remains of rush-hour traffic, and get him safely to his elegant brownstone on the Eastside. X's head, eyes still shaded behind those disarming sunglasses, lolls to one side.

Go for it, Roxi. You know how to handle sleeping passengers.

But this isn't just any sleeping passenger. This is a man who literally leaves me breathless. I cannot concentrate when I am around him. I am weak-kneed.

Reaching over, I gently touch X's shoulder. It produces a slight exhalation. A taxi honks behind us and he is jolted awake.

"Have we arrived?" he asks, his accented voice husky with sleep.

"Yes, you are home."

He gets out of the car and I pop the trunk. By the

time I make it around to the back, his bags are on the sidewalk beside him.

"Invoice Alexandra as you usually do," X says, folding something into my palm. Before I can protest he takes off and does not look back.

I am mortified. I've just been treated like a chauffeur. In the past, X has handled gratuities in a much more diplomatic manner. They've been added to the bill by his assistant, Alexandra, who pays me by international money order.

Feeling lower than a deflated tire, I heave myself back into the driver's seat. Taking a deep breath I open my palm. How much am I worth to him?

I am holding an expensive cream-colored business card in my hand. I have X's real name and telephone number.

"Carlo DeAngelo," I say aloud, liking the sound.

Carlo and Roxanne DeAngelo, even better. I am ahead of myself, jumping the gun.

I have two hours to think what this means while I drive back to Long Island, shower and dress for a date.

This one's a recently divorced man and supposedly someone my friend's husband works out with.

It's a blind date.

Yes, yes, I know. I am definitely a glutton for punishment.

CHAPTER 4

"So what is it you do?" I ask the man across the table from me. We are seated in a cozy banquette at a Caribbean restaurant on the north shore of Long Island. So far the food is good and the customers decked out in expensive designer gear are upscale. Service has been impeccable up to now.

"A little of this and a little of that," Jeff, my date says. "But primarily I sell medical equipment."

I translate that to mean he is unemployed or still figuring out what he wants to do. Jeff is tall, fortysomething, in good shape, and judging by the way he positions things, thinks highly of himself. A red flag is already fluttering. I've already been left cooling my heels for a good fifteen minutes at the bar. About to leave, he'd finally showed up and didn't even bother to apologize.

"Roxanne!" he announces loudly enough for the entire restaurant to hear. "Hugo and Betsy's description of you hardly does you justice." Then he links an arm through mine as if we are a couple. I guess he decided I was presentable or he would simply have left me sitting there.

We are whisked to a secluded banquette by the host before a waiter comes over to take our order.

Jeff continues his running commentary. I am supposed to be impressed by his portfolio. Since I haven't been able to get in a word I nod and act as if I'm hooked.

"Do you like to dance?" he asks.

"Love to."

Finally I've been able to say something.

"Good. Then that's settled. I know a wonderful jazz club we can go to afterward."

He is taking control, trying to manage the evening and have it come out his way. My attention turns to the menu. We order. Jeff is still talking, telling me what he owns, the types of vacations he enjoys. Yada, yada, yada.

The grandstanding continues while we wait for the meal. All the while I am conscious of Jeff looking me over. I already know we will not be a love connection. He is a man of a certain age and badly in need of validation. I don't have the personality to flatter or give him constant reassurance. Nor will I allow him to always get his way.

"The last woman I dated was frigid," Jeff says out of the blue.

I pause in the middle of spearing my Jerk Steak. "She was?" I mean, what else is there to say. I wait for him to explain.

"She actually thanked me for not putting pressure on her. She wanted me to wait before we had sex."

What an obnoxious man. How am I going to make it through this meal?

"Does that make her frigid or careful?" I ask.

Jeff's jaw muscles tighten. He hates that I call him on it. Too damn bad.

"No one waits five dates anymore," he says through clenched teeth. "Not if they want things to work."

"I would if I had concerns about the man or just wasn't interested."

Jeff clears his throat and tries to make light of it. "Are you saying you have concerns about me? Or should I have concerns about you?"

How to answer that? "I don't really know you," I say, hedging. "I just know what Betsy and Hugo tell me about you."

Betsy is my old college pal. Hugo is her third husband. He is an entrepreneur and hugely successful. They work well together. I've long suspected that Betsy, a lawyer, is the one bringing in the income and Hugo provides window dressing. He is a good-looking man and in perfect shape. Hugo and Jeff are supposedly gym buddies and Jeff is a regular guest at Hugo and Betsy's dinner table, or so I've been told.

"How long have you been divorced?" I ask.

"Three months."

I hike an eyebrow. "And you're ready to date?"

It is not a fair comment especially since I put myself out there almost immediately. By the time you summon up the courage to ask for a divorce you've been mentally divorced for years. The papers are just a formality.

My date doesn't blink. "My philosophy is brush yourself off and move on. Women are a dime a dozen. They come and they go. At this stage of life I'm not expecting butterflies to flutter, I'm just looking for commonalities."

Nice guy. Practical, too. As long as she's breathing that's good enough for him.

"I'm expecting butterflies," I say, and wait for his reaction.

Warning to the not so wise, stay away from a guy like Jeff who thinks women are a dime a dozen. He has *user* and maybe *player* written all over his handsome face. I make a mental note to have a nice long talk with Hugo and Betsy when I get home. And home is where I plan to be as soon as I finish my meal.

"You're not drinking your wine," Jeff points out ignoring my comment.

And for good reason. I want all my senses about me

when I make a quick departure. I oblige Jeff by taking a tiny sip.

"Hugo says you were married for fifteen years. That's a long time. What happened?" he asks.

I resent the personal questions. Some things I will not and cannot discuss with strangers. Besides it's none of his business.

"Life happened," I answer, my eyes on my cooling dinner. I've lost my appetite. I already know Jeff is clearly not for me, and I am definitely not for him so why are we wasting each other's time. He needs a "fun" girl; someone living in the here and now and not looking to make a connection. And I need to make it through dinner and make my way home.

"That's a rather vague answer," he persists.

Vague or not that is all he is getting.

"We grew apart." I wonder what he will do if I turn the tables on him so I do. "What happened with your relationship?"

"Which one?"

Oh, boy, I've opened a can of worms. Not that his answer has come as any big surprise.

"The most recent one."

"Oh, Tracey. She was my third wife. In retrospect I realize I might have married her on the rebound. She was too demanding. It wasn't a good time in my life."

Demanding means Tracey asked questions Jeff didn't want to answer. As I had picked up on earlier, he is used to getting his way. Imagine being on a third wife and not yet forty.

Yawning, I make a production of covering my mouth. "It's been a long day."

Jeff pretends not to hear.

"You own your own business. That's impressive. I bet you scare away a lot of men."

I want to scare *him* away.

"Only if they're not secure," I shoot back.

He smiles. He is all bluster. "You don't scare me. I like an independent woman."

I bet he does. And I bet he is hoping I'll pick up the dinner tab, too. I can be persuaded if it means an end to the dismal evening. I've had just about enough of Jeff.

"How about we pass on dessert and head for the jazz club I mentioned earlier?" he suggests.

I yawn again, loudly, hoping he'll get the message this time. "Sorry, like I said, it's been a long day."

Jeff's clenched jaw indicates he is none too pleased. When he signals for the check I decide to let him pay. As obnoxious as he is, it is only fitting.

When we stand outside waiting for the valet there is an awkward silence.

Jeff tries again. "Sure you don't want to go dancing?"

"I'm sure."

Nodding coolly, he tips the driver who brings around a black Infiniti. With a wave of his hand he takes off.

I am learning to trust my instincts more and more and I'm listening to that inner voice. I'd driven my own car to the restaurant tonight for a reason. Having your own wheels ensures you're in control. If I'd been dependent on Jeff for transportation it would not have been good.

What could Betsy and Hugo have been thinking of?

But I am nothing if not polite. Next day when I power on my laptop and check my messages, I send Jeff a quick e thanking him for dinner. He has after all paid. Plus, it is the right thing to do.

Then I go about my business. I have a breakfast meeting with three of my employees, all students. This is a standing engagement every Wednesday. I use this opportunity to update them on any changes and give them the next week's schedule. Other than that we communicate via e-mail.

The diner where we usually meet is right off the Southern State Parkway. It is one of those mom-and-pop operations that's been around forever. The waitresses are all fixtures and the food, though not fancy, is filling. The owners treat everyone as if they are the only customers in the place. Me they treat like a queen.

The moment I walk in, Connie, the hostess, greets me like long-lost family.

"How ya doing, hon? Your friends are seated already." She points a crimson talon at a booth in the back.

Connie has one of those annoying outer-borough accents that makes all her *A*'s sound like *O*'s. She has big platinum blond hair that frames her face in ringlets and thick black eyeliner rimming her eyes. I try not to laugh but she does remind me of an ageing Orphan Annie.

Vance, Kazoo and Lydia, who are my staff, are already working their way through the bread basket. Vance is an African American like me and wears his hair in long cornrows secured back with a thong. He stands when he sees me coming. Despite his less-than-conservative appearance, his mama has brought him up well. He is a gentleman and as polite as can be.

Lydia who is as white bread as they come is busy holding court. She is one of those porcelain blondes who looks as if she might fall over if you stare at her too hard. But don't underestimate the woman. I've seen her sling a forty-pound sack of dog food over one shoulder and carry it around like tissue paper. Lydia takes the train in from Connecticut for meetings and to perform jobs requiring more than a computer.

Rounding out my threesome of students is Kazoo,

a naturalized U.S. citizen who hails from Japan. Kazoo is my rock, trustworthy, always dependable and a good problem solver.

"Hey, Roxi, how's it going?" Vance greets, holding out a vacant chair until I slide into it.

I thank him and sit. My smart pumps that I think are so stylish are beginning to pinch. I slap down my Coach briefcase on the Formica table and ask, "Has anyone ordered coffee?"

"I did." Lydia's voice is modulated, cultured. Her folks came over with the Mayflower if I were to hazard a guess.

The waitress, a pretty dark-haired Latin woman hurries toward us, two pots in hand. She is a mind reader. She sets them down, fumbles through her pockets and hands me a menu.

"Has everyone else ordered?" I ask.

"We did," Kazoo says.

Normally I keep my weekly meetings to two hours; after that no one pays attention. I stab a finger at the first items on the menu.

"I'll have oatmeal, a toasted bagel with a dab of butter and one egg over easy."

"Be back in a jiffy," the waitress says, ambling off.

I ignore the pot marked Decaf and reach for the real stuff. I pour a cup that will put hair on my chest, add cream, none of that low-fat stuff for me, and a packet of Equal.

Vance, who doesn't drink coffee, has brought his own teabag, which he takes from his backpack. He pours a cup of water and plops the bag in. Lydia reaches for the decaf and fills her cup.

I take a big gulp of coffee before passing out next week's schedule. With the Thanksgiving holiday just around the corner, business is starting to pick up. I have a long list of people who need shopping done, some even require a meal cooked and served.

Typically this time of year is my busiest. People always need house-sitting and pet-care services. It is the time of year when some real money comes in.

I am in the midst of negotiating with Lydia who wants a week off, but had forgotten to mention it before, when a voice comes over my shoulder.

"Marina, good to see you."

The voice has a familiar ring to it. Busted! Marina is one of my online names. My crew stares at me waiting for an explanation. I don't want anyone knowing I have a cyber life.

I glance over my shoulder and can't immediately place the hulk smiling down at me.

"Rick, remember?"

A vague memory surfaces. He is the guy who

claimed to be a hospital administrator. Although he doesn't look like any administrator I know. After several e-mails Rick and I met at a diner; a place similar to this almost eight months ago. Rick had shown up all sinew and bulging muscles, in a muscle shirt and track pants. Gross. I mean, this is a first date, you are supposed to dress to impress.

I'd taken one look at him and determined he was not for me. We'd talked for a few minutes and although he seemed to be a perfectly nice guy, I couldn't get past that first impression. Those fleeting first moments are ever so crucial. Intelligent or not, I hated the Joe Jock look.

"Marina?" Rick repeats again in case I haven't heard him. "I can't believe I've run into you."

"Marina," Lydia repeats, sounding puzzled. Her gaze alternates between me and Rick. "Roxi, you're holding out on us. Is that your real name?"

I wish she'd shut the hell up. I've protected my identity fiercely and she's blown it in just a few seconds.

Rick leers down at me as if seeing me made his day. Today he is fully clothed and those bulging biceps are hidden in winter garb.

"Marina, why didn't you answer my e-mails? You never returned my calls. Did I say something? Do something?"

I stand up and place a hand on one of those corded biceps. When I lead him away from the group he is still jabbering about how he thought I was deliberately trying to dump him. Maybe he isn't so dumb after all.

"Look, Rick, I'm in the middle of a meeting. Can I call you later?"

"Sure. Call my cell phone."

Rick and I had spent less than an hour during our initial meeting together. For some that might seem a short time but to me it felt like days. We'd had coffee and I'd downed my drink as quickly as possible, glad that we'd not made plans for dinner.

Rick's physical appearance just does not do it for me. I like my men more understated.

"I'll call you," I say, all wide-eyed and sincere, although fat chance of that happening.

"You still have my number?"

"Of course."

"Who was that?" Lydia asks after he leaves.

"A friend."

Vance looks skeptical but keeps his mouth shut.

We resume our discussion and focus on the week's schedule. Lydia, manipulative as ever, is doing a lot of talking. She is working on getting the guys to pick up her slack so that she can have the week off to go to her family's place on the Cape.

Kazoo who has been more fidgety than I ever remember drops a bomb.

"I have to give two weeks' notice," he says, shifting
uncomfortably.

"Why?" I ask, concerned that maybe there is a family crisis he hasn't discussed.

"I've accepted another job."

I hadn't seen it coming. From the expression on everyone else's faces, none of us had. Kazoo has never
indicated he is unhappy. He is reliable and dependable and I take him for granted. I count on him
because he always does what he is supposed to, never
once complaining, and he resolves problems with
minimal help.

"You can't abandon us," Lydia wails. "We're a
team. Walking out on us is not an option." Lydia
sounds as if she is about to get hysterical. I suspect that
Kazoo has picked up a lot of her slack and now she is
panicked.

Kazoo, remorseful, hangs his head.

"Who with?" I pry.

"A new business starting up."

I am instantly on the alert. "What new business?"

I think he is ungrateful. Kazoo's appearance initially
did not inspire confidence. But I kept an open mind
and he turned out to be a nice surprise. My soon-to-

be-ex-employee has silver hair with black streaks and piercings everywhere. His arms and legs are wreathed in tattoos and he wears homeboy clothes.

Kazoo can't meet my eyes. I'm not about to let him off the hook.

"Who owns this new business?"

His eyes dart left then right. "SNI."

"You're kidding! Service Not Incidental!" Lydia snorts. She sounds totally outraged. "That's a new start-up operation."

I step in. "Kazoo, I wish you'd spoken to me before accepting."

He shutters his eyes. "I tried to, but they offered me more money."

"Who are they?"

Kazoo's mouth opens and then closes. Vance and Lydia wait to see what I'm going to do. We wait. Nothing more from Kazoo.

"Okay, I'll accept your resignation as of today," I say, taking charge.

"But I'm giving you two weeks notice, Roxi," Kazoo pleads, sounding surprised that I am not ecstatic about him moving on.

"Thank you but that's not necessary. You no longer have a job." I turn to Vance and Lydia for support. "If you know anyone who can take Kazoo's place have them contact me. I'll take on his duties until we find a replacement."

Gathering my paperwork, I shove it into my brief-case. I am really pissed. Someone is infringing on my territory and pilfering my employees.

And I am bent and determined to find out who owns SNI.

CHAPTER 5

The moment I get home I begin calling everyone I know. But no one in my immediate circle seems to know who the owners of Service Not Incidental are. I begin punching in the numbers of business acquaintances I haven't spoken to in years, hoping that someone might have a clue. I am willing to do just about anything to find out what I need to know. This is my livelihood we are talking about.

Since no one knows anything, or if they do are reluctant to say, I am left with one option, call the company myself or find someone to call for me. I pick up the phone and call Margot.

"Yes, Roxi?" she says as if she's been expecting me.

From the sound of her voice, Margot is on a high right now which means she's been in contact with Earl. I decide to take advantage of her good mood before it passes.

"I need you to do me a favor," I say.

"Sure. As long as it doesn't require me getting into a car. I'm at the beauty salon getting my hair relaxed."

I tell her what I've heard and what I need.

"No problem. Give me a few minutes and I'll get back to you."

While I wait for Margot to call me back I turn on my laptop and scan my e-mail messages. I am feeling pretty good. I've picked up some new clients. I shoot them my standard welcome e-mail introducing myself and telling them what they can expect from my service. I attach a copy of my contract and zap the messages into cyber-space.

I go surfing, find a job site where I can post an ad, and describe that I need a friendly and dedicated customer-service type. I've learned a long time ago that experience does not necessarily mean service ori-entated. Attitude is not something you can train. I can't just sit back and wait for my employees, Vance or Lydia, to find me help. In today's world the only person you can rely on is yourself.

I've just posted my ad when my cell phone rings. I check caller ID. Margot is already getting back to me.

"What did you find out?" I quiz, before she can get the first word out.

"You know a Karen Miller or Tamara Fisher?"

"They sound vaguely familiar." I am thinking.

"They're the owners of Service Not Incidental."

It clicks. I remember now.

"Those lowdown dirty…" I swallow the cussword before it escapes. Talk about feeling betrayed.

Karen Miller and Tamara Fisher were graduate students at Hofstra when I hired them a year or so ago. Their schedules weren't that flexible and neither had worked with the public before. But they were bright, enthusiastic and definitely trainable, and I am a sucker for the underdog. I'd given them a shot and this is how they are paying me back.

Why did I do it? Because I know what it's like to be a starving college student. I have a starving college student of my own. I'd been flexible and accommodating with their schedules. I've always thought black folks should help each other out. Give each other a jumpstart.

Less than three months later, Karen quit claiming she couldn't keep up with her schoolwork. Tamara lasted another six weeks and then just disappeared. I'd been happy to see the last of her. She'd had one too many customer complaints and a history of absences. I hadn't seen or heard from either since.

"Where did they set up shop?" I snap, irritated that these two young women I helped were now competing against me.

"You're not going to like this," Margot warns sounding cagey.

"Just tell me."

"In Hempstead."

"That's practically next door! First they steal one of my employees and now they're after my customers."

This time I let the cuss words rip.

"Don't take my head off, I'm just the messenger. They're offering a twenty-percent discount certificate to anyone signing up for their services. And they're offering a holiday gift of one service free. 'Course that service has a price limit."

I cuss again. Now I need to come one better.

These women are trying to put me out of business. I have to create my own marketing promotion and fast.

"I made an appointment to come in and see their operation," Margot said, loyal as ever and thinking ahead. "I told them I couldn't commit to anything unless I met them in person."

"You rock, girl. Don't tell me they have offices."

"Yup, in a renovated old house. In case you need it I wrote down the address and directions."

Karen and Tamara are definitely out to give me a run for my money. I have a home office, and it sounds as if they have rental space. Whenever I meet a client, I arrange to have lunch or coffee at a restaurant, so what I want to know is where a start-up business gets the money to lease an office, usually you need to cut down on overhead.

They've taken out loans I guess, but it still galls me. It took me two years to make a profit on my business. And I'm still in no position to rent office space much less a whole house.

Through clenched teeth I grind out, "Check the place out for me and ask lots of questions."

"You know I will."

The conversation shifts to other things. We begin to talk about the dinner party Margot invited me to on Christmas Day. It is one of those deals where you bring along a single friend. Since someone else invited her, I am the "single" friend.

"We need to go shopping and get something hot to wear," Margot suggests, her voice high.

It doesn't take much coaxing. Shopping has always been a favorite pastime of mine. Some people eat when they're pissed. Not me, I shop.

"Anyone at this dinner party worth meeting?" I ask.

"If you mean men, Keisha claims she met a doctor at something similar."

"Keisha meets men when she's taking out the garbage."

Margot's friend dresses like a "ho," and acts like a "ho." Her clothes are so tight they look like a second skin. If her boobs aren't hanging out, then it isn't worth wearing.

"How about we meet in a couple of hours? I should be out from under the dryer by then," Margot adds.

She's never been one to let grass grow under her feet. The wheels are already grinding away in her head, and she is probably fantasizing about the doctor she thinks she will meet.

"I'm thinking animal-print skirt and an off-the-shoulder sweater, maybe earrings that skim my shoulders, wonder if I should wear tights with my boots?" Margot jabbers, in one of her famous run-on sentences, "Warm, rich colors look good on me."

"Who's driving?" I ask.

"Me. I'll swing by and pick you up."

My cell phone rings. A customer, hopefully.

Sadie DeVila is on the line. She is a big mucka-mucka with a software company and a major pain in the ass. Since Sadie spends most of her life on the road, she frequently needs my services. Usually she is looking for a house sitter to pick up the mail, water the plants and give the impression her place is occupied. Those jobs are usually tailor-made for Lydia. After I get done with Sadie I send Lydia a quick e-mail.

I return a few phone calls from messages left earlier and then I check on those jobs that Kazoo was supposed to be handling. Luckily I have a handful of back-up employees on standby for situations like this.

I call four before I finally get lucky. One of the women has just graduated college and is looking for a job. That means she needs money. I dangle the possibility of a permanent position in front of her and she bites.

That takes care of one issue. Now it's back to checking my personal e-mail. E-mail gets pretty addictive when you're listed on a dating site. You're pumped when someone new contacts you because you think each new prospect brings you one step closer to finding Mr. Right.

I read my mail dutifully and scan the respective profiles and photos. None are going to set me on fire. But I respond anyway, giving the Cliff's Notes version of my life. Then it's back to work I go, making sure groceries are delivered to a client in Garden City.

I check to make sure the plants at the Millers' are watered and the housekeeper is doing what she is supposed to do. Now I still have an hour to kill before Margot shows up. I decide to take a nap and turn off the ringer on the phones, leaving the answering machine to pick up.

What seems minutes later, I awake with the roar of a freight train running through my head. I punch the snooze button, glance at the bedside clock and damn near have a stroke. I am about to screw up royally, but at least Margot is late. I run a marathon getting dressed.

While I am putting on my makeup, a horn blasts out front.

I stick my head out the window letting in the chill November air and yell, "I'm coming." Margot is sitting swaddled in furs behind the wheel of her Lexus. Around her, kids zip by on Rollerblades trying to get an evasive hockey puck into the net. The game is fast and furious.

Malverne is one of these neighborhoods that draws both the middle and upper-middle class. It is home to executives sick of city living and those who prefer a simpler life with less stress. It is not normally a place where single women live. But I got the house and I have no plans of moving. We're a mixed community, though whites outnumber blacks. But we're cool here and race is not a major issue.

Lindsay, my daughter, grew up in Malverne playing lacrosse and hockey along with basketball and soccer. She's had sleepovers with kids of every ethnicity and she knows just about everyone in town and vice versa.

Margot toots her horn again. This time I go flying out of the front door belting my leather coat, the strap of a Coach purse slung over my shoulder. I climb into the Lexus and angle my cheek for Margot's air kiss. Eyes closed, I lie back on the headrest. "Whoosh!"

"What took you so long?" she growls once I am settled.

"I fell asleep. Pardon me for being human. Where are we heading?"

"Roosevelt Field."

And with that we zoom off.

Three hours later we are still trudging around the mall, arms laden with packages and feet beginning to ache.

"We need to stop somewhere and get something cool to drink," I suggest.

We head into one of those fast-food joints that malls are famous for and take a seat. I order a milk shake—I deserve it I figure—and Margot orders coffee and a chunk of red-velvet cake. The place actually has it on the menu which surprises me.

"I'm worried about this new company starting up," I admit after I've had several slurps.

"Why? You're established. You've got a name."

Margot is only saying this to make me feel better.

"There are two of them and one of me. Those women know how Wife for Hire works," I wail.

"They're rookies. You know how to soothe the most difficult customers, and you're expert at resolving issues in a diplomatic way."

I feel better. Margot, neurotic as she can be, suffers from the loyalty trait. You don't find that in too many people these days.

We talk about the outfits we've just bought and what would go with what. Then we convince ourselves we need shoes and cosmetics to really make them work. It turns into an evening of retail therapy and very well deserved. By the time Margot drops me off I am dragging.

As soon as I walk into my house I spot the blinking red light on the answering machine and groan. I kick off my shoes, pour myself a glass of wine and decide that I might as well get it over with and find out who I have to call back.

It's Rick Jones, the guy I'd run into at the diner earlier. Unbelievable he still has my number.

"Hey, princess," he croons. "Sure was nice to see you again. I almost forgot how fine you are. I'd really like for us to get together. If you name a place I'll take you there."

When hell freezes over.

Rick rattles off at least three different numbers where he can be reached. None of which I write down.

I hit the erase button and that is that.

Next I hear my baby's voice and my heart rises in my throat. My child is everything to me.

"Ma..." When Lindsay calls me 'Ma' it means she

is in trouble. "Ma…I'm coming home earlier than planned. I need to talk to you."

Lindsay is supposed to be home in a week on her Thanksgiving vacation. Now she's coming home earlier. My mind races examining all the possibilities. Is she dropping out of college? Is she pregnant? Or is she moving in with the boyfriend she's been dating for six months? They all seem pretty horrible to me.

I glance at the clock on the mantelpiece. It is late, but this can't wait until the morning. I pick up the phone and call Lindsay's cell phone. When voice mail kicks in I leave a message. I call her dorm but the phone in her room rings and rings. Now I am even more upset.

I gulp my glass of wine, head for bed and try counting sheep.

Sleep is supposed to be an antidote when life gets in the way. But tonight sleep is not happening. I need to hear my child's voice. I will be a raving lunatic until I do.

CHAPTER 6

Lindsay's car is in the driveway when I wake up. Without brushing my teeth I hurry to her room, preparing to shake sense into her if I have to. Squaring my shoulders, I take a deep breath before tapping on her bedroom door. I have no idea what time she got in last evening nor do I care. She owes me an explanation for why she is here.

I get no response so I knock again, this time louder. When that doesn't work, I turn the doorknob and stick my head through the crack.

"Lindsay, baby, wake up, Mom's here!"

A gentle snore comes from under the covers. That child is sleeping the sleep of the dead. She's wound the sheets and comforter around her mummy-style and she looks like a butterfly waiting to come out of a cocoon.

I sit on the edge of her bed and begin stroking her back through the bulky comforter. Lindsay's breathing doesn't change. This isn't a game. The child is dead to the world. Guilt kicks in. I really should let her rest. Then I reason I am her mother. I've been heartsick since getting that message and scared to death. I need to know what is going on.

"Lindsay!" I shout, this time louder. "Wake up, love."

She stirs under the heavy comforter and sighs.

"Lindsay! Get up this minute!"

"Ma, can't it wait."

"No, it can't wait. I want to know why you're home. I didn't expect you until next week."

"I'll talk over breakfast, Ma. Make me pancakes?"

She sounds like a little girl, my little girl. Lindsay has always loved pancakes. I wonder why the delaying tactic. This is making me more nervous by the minute.

"You've got fifteen minutes to wash up and be at the table," I say.

One blood-red eye shoots open.

"All right, Ma." A noisy yawn follows.

"Fifteen minutes, Lin."

With that I march out and slam the door.

Lindsay is ten minutes later than the fifteen I have given her. But at least she is here, seated and slumped over, sipping on the mug of coffee I have set down.

I flip a couple of pancakes onto her plate and place bacon on the side. She reaches for the pitcher of syrup, pouring a copious amount on her cakes. It is a wonder the child stays so slim.

People say we look alike. I've always thought Lindsay looks more like her father, handsome player that he is. She is much more slender than me and has a waiflike look to her. There isn't an excess ounce of fat on that child.

But we are both high-energy people, our minds constantly racing, our hands constantly doing. Lindsay has smooth caramel–colored skin and tight bouncy curls— that frame a heart-shaped face. She has amber eyes and a smile that is engaging; it literally pulls you right in. That smile is usually a permanent fixture, but not today.

"What's going on?" I ask her when she makes no attempt to initiate conversation.

Lindsay sets down her fork and looks at me. "You're not going to like what I have to say, Ma."

"Try me."

"You better sit down then."

I sink into a chair before my knees buckle. Please tell me the child isn't pregnant.

"I'm waiting, Lindsay."

Lindsay puts down her knife and lines it up with her fork. Now I know things are serious. Lin is not what you would call meticulous.

"I'm taking off for a year, Ma. I'm leaving the country."

My heart lodges in my mouth, my gut wants to spill the few bites of breakfast I have taken. "Taking off, as in dropping out of school?"

"Not dropping out, taking a break."

"Lindsay! I can't support your choice."

"You don't have to. It's already done. I'm going to Paris."

"Paris! Why Paris?"

"Because I want to give modeling a try."

The room sways then steadies around me. I take a deep breath and try putting things in perspective. At least she isn't trekking across the Himalayas or taking off on safari with some loser. She isn't running off with a boyfriend she's known for six months. And thank you, Jesus, she isn't pregnant.

I'm still not happy, but what can I do?

"What are you proposing to live on while you're there?" I ask.

"I'll get paid, plus I have savings from my part-time job. I'll be living with a family taking care of their two children until my modeling career takes off."

"You're going to be an au pair? That's what I sent you to school for?"

"I want to speak French fluently, Ma. Living with a family takes care of major expenses until I get established."

She has it all planned out. My shoulders sag and I gulp in a breath. It isn't so bad. My child will live with a family and hopefully be protected and cared for. Hopefully that family is a stable, functional one. She'll get paid a salary, and if she gets lucky might even have a new career.

In some ways, I envy her. A lifetime ago, it seems I was young, carefree and thought I could take on the world. Now I am happy to be alive, in good health and with a business that pays the bills.

I place an arm around Lindsay's shoulders and kiss her cheek.

"If it makes you happy, baby, go live in Paris. It's every woman's dream."

But even as I give her my blessing I already feel the loss. What if she falls in love with the city and never comes home?

You have to cut the ties sometime. Lindsay is nineteen. She's always had a good head on her shoulders. I need to let her go without guilt or recrimination. But all I want to do is hug her and cry.

Lindsay stands and places her plate and cup in the sink. She does an elegant neck roll. Her wild black curls are standing straight up, and her honey complexion has a tinge of rose to it. She is still only half-awake, I can tell.

"You think I can go back to bed now, Ma?" she asks, glancing at the kitchen clock. "I only had three hours sleep and it was a long drive."

"Of course."

I have things to take care of myself. I want to speak to my banker about the possibility of a loan. I'll need money for marketing. I am also beginning to think that maybe it is time Wife for Hire has an office outside of my home.

We go our separate ways. Lindsay back to bed and me to Chase Bank.

After an hour of grilling by one of the vice presidents of the bank I leave feeling optimistic. I've never been much of a borrower but maybe it is time to expand. Wife for Hire was started with my own savings. And I've always prided myself on having minimal overhead. It is time to adjust my thinking.

I will need a major advertising campaign to keep abreast of the competition. That kind of thing costs money. Money I do not have. But if I can bring in more business and hire more people, I will be able to pay off this loan in little or no time.

I have a client's Jaguar to pick up from the shop. It is one of those jobs I've not been able to delegate, as he trusts me implicitly. My head still filled with marketing ideas, I drive to the Jaguar dealership in nearby Valley Stream. After parking my Land Rover, I drive his vehicle back to his house and the dealership's courtesy transportation picks me up.

I am plowing through the parking lot of the dealership at a pretty rapid speed, looking for the exit, when I am forced to brake quickly. Heart palpitating, I roll down my window.

"You jerk. What if I'd run you over?" I ask a man who has popped out of nowhere. Then I feel bad for yelling. What if his car has broken down and he's looking for help?

He stares at me with a silly smile on his mug.

"Is something wrong?" I ask as he comes closer and I hit the button until my window is almost up. He could be a lunatic.

"No, things couldn't be better." He presses his nose against the window pane and says in a deep voice, "I saw you get into your car. I wanted to meet you."

I should be flattered, instead I am wary. He is presentable enough in his expensive black wool coat and leather gloves. But what does he really want?

"You were willing to risk being run over?" I ask, "Because you wanted to meet me?"

"I knew you would stop."

Cocky. Every bone screams player!

A business card sails onto the passenger seat next to me. "Call me sometime, will ya?"

HOOK, LINE AND SINGLE   77

He *is* crazy. This is New York. He could be a serial killer for all I know.

Like a bat out of hell, I peel out of there. I have a few more errands to run and then I'm taking the rest of the afternoon off to spend with Lindsay. We'll have a late lunch and maybe take in a movie.

I am slowly beginning to come to terms with Lindsay's decision. And I am determined to spend as much time with her as possible before she leaves. She is at a critical time in her life and still needs her mother. Or so I convince myself.

When I pull into my driveway it looks as if there is a party on the block. Cars are parked in every available slot and rap music comes from inside my house. The neighbors must be fuming.

In my absence, Lindsay has decided to have a party. I enter to find her friends lounged around my home-entertainment center, munching on popcorn and chips.

"Hello, Ms. Ingram," they greet in unison.

"Where's Lindsay?"

Several fingers point to the kitchen before heads bopping they return to their music.

My baby is frowning, concentrating on something on the stove. She has whipped up some snack but I can't tell exactly what from the smell.

"What's going on?" I ask, my arms folded.

"Ma, most of my friends can't afford to go away to college. We see each other when we can. We're just hanging out. You know everyone here."

On second glance, I recognize several who were fixtures when Lindsay was living at home. I soften.

"Have fun, baby. I'll make myself scarce and give you guys your space."

When I begin walking away, Lindsay stands in my path. She throws her arms around me, squeezing so hard I barely can breathe.

"Thanks for being understanding, Mom. You've always encouraged me to have an adventurous spirit. If nothing comes of this modeling business at least I can say I tried it."

I hug her to me. "I'll always support your choices, love. Always. I have your back. Just promise me you'll get a degree. You'll need something to fall back on if this doesn't work out."

"I promise I'll graduate college. I love you, Mom." Lindsay gives me another squeeze. Her promise is all I can ask for.

Before I make a total fool of myself I head for the staircase. Upstairs in private I can cry.

My mother was never this supportive. She comes from a time when women didn't dare dream. She kept drumming into my head to be content with what I have, regardless of how little. While I might have been content, I was always hungry and I had big dreams. And even though I got pregnant at nineteen I didn't let that hold me back.

I was born an overachiever. I saved the few pennies I had for an allowance to open up my first lemonade stand. Then I took the profits and started a neighborhood car-washing business. When I was too pregnant to work, the money I got from Kane, my ex-husband, I saved. And I went back to college as soon as I could, because I knew without a degree I was powerless.

But now I am beginning to think the world is conspiring against me. My business is at risk. My daughter is leaving for a foreign land. I need a break?

I have one foot on the top step when my cell phone rings.

"Roxanne Ingram," I say in my business voice.

A woman sounds damn close to being hysterical. It takes some effort to make out what she's saying, but trust me it's not good.

"I can be in Lawrence in fifteen minutes," I say in a rush.

The clown; that lovely rotund man I hired to entertain at a four-year-old's party is scaring the kids. The mother wants him gone.

I make the drive to the Five Towns area in ten minutes flat. I am there in time to see tearful mothers rushing to their cars tugging kids by the hand.

On the front lawn, an obviously inebriated clown is being sat on by the birthday boy's dad and a man I presume is a neighbor. They are pummeling him in the hopes he will stop singing "Happy Birthday."

This is going to cost me big-time. I leap into action, apologizing profusely and taking full responsibility for the debacle. I had checked the clown's references and he had come up clean. But no one wants to hear that right now.

Eventually the clown is taken home to dry out by a tearful and apologetic wife. The client is reimbursed for the entire party and I promise to pay for a puppet show in the coming week. The whole thing sets me back several hundred dollars.

A small price to pay if I don't get sued. It sure looks as if the world is conspiring against me.

I decide to drive over to Margot's. I need comforting and soothing.

CHAPTER 7

The next few weeks go by, and business comes in dribs and drabs. Since Thanksgiving is fast approaching, things are bound to pick up. I see John, the ex-military guy, my only match from speed dating a few times. But the more I see him the less interested I am, and a good thing, too, because he turns out to be a weirdo.

He keeps insisting on afternoon dates and always seems to have someplace to be afterward. I am beginning to suspect he might be married or just cheap. One day out of the blue he e-mails to tell me he thinks we should be friends. Right after that announcement he begins calling again.

I've played therapist for more than my share of men and I've vowed I would never do it again. Listening to all that drama about the ex done them wrong saps your energy and makes you irritable. In the end what you have is a dependent man who can't cope with life's ups and downs. Been there. Done that. Wouldn't do it again. Let John invest in a therapist.

The phone rings. It is Margot with an invitation to Thanksgiving dinner. She wants me to bring Lindsay along. It will be six of us, including the couple next door and Margot's niece from out of town who invited herself.

Margot isn't a great cook but she is smart enough to know it. She has the Thanksgiving meal catered by a local restaurant. That afternoon we sit around downing large goblets of wine. Wine makes it that much easier to be with people you barely know especially when you're single.

I make it through the day telling myself this is fun. With Thanksgiving over with, preparations for Christmas begin. I am starting to worry about my business. I want the competition out of the way.

Margot comes back from meeting Karen Miller and Tamara Fisher, the owners of Service Not Incidental, all elated. I am pissed. She is impressed with their operation and talks nonstop about their facility. I question her relentlessly and take notes, but I am resentful and angry and feel used. How can two young women, fresh out of college, afford a renovated Victorian home and all the trimmings?

Margot had been offered beverages and snacks while they interviewed her. She'd been given a tour of the business and shown their state-of-the-art computer equipment, complete with customer-relationship-management software. Service Not Incidental is all about personalized service they say. There the customer reigns.

Margot doesn't have one negative word to report. Her description makes me want to see the operation myself. I plan to drive by their business later just to see what is going on. I decide to take a deep breath and calm down. I continue checking my e-mails, alternating back and forth between personal and business until the phone rings.

"Wife for Hire. This is Roxanne."

"Ms. Ingram, this is Alexandra calling on behalf of Mr. Carlo DeAngelo."

My heart literally skips a beat. I've moved up in the world. Mr. X's assistant has identified him by name. Usually Alexandra calls on behalf of DeAngelo Creations, which leaves a lot of room for your imagination. I mean, what exactly does he create?

I clutch the receiver and listen to a long list of duties Mr. X needs help with. I am already calculating how much each will cost. This is an unexpected Christmas bonus, and much needed I might add. I want to kiss the man.

"There's also something else Mr. DeAngelo would like help with," Alexandra says.

"Name it," I say excitedly.

"He'd like you to take care of Bacci."

"Bacci?"

"His cat. He's Mr. DeAngelo's pride and joy."

X has a cat? If anything I picture him with a dog; an exotic breed like an Afghan or English Boxer. A cat doesn't seem to go with him, but a pet says he is human. Of course there is no way I am going to turn down this opportunity.

"What kind of cat is Bacci?" I ask, just so Alexandra will know I was listening and am interested.

"A stray. Mr. DeAngelo found him starved and almost frozen to death going through his garbage cans."

"He rescued him?" I am in love. This humane side of Carlo is very appealing. He'd saved a poor starving cat from God knew what. My imagination takes over. I see us saving hundreds of cats and setting up a sanctuary for those lost or about to be euthanized. We will be the savior of animals. We will open a business together.

"Shall I tell Mr. DeAngelo you'll take care of Bacci, then?" his assistant asks.

"Sure."

I have no plans yet for the Christmas holiday, except for dinner, and a cat can be left for an hour or two. While caring for a cat is not in the plan, I can make this work to my advantage.

I have a sudden brainstorm. "Tell you what," I say. "Tell Mr. DeAngelo I'll take care of Bacci in my own home. Can someone bring him to me?"

"I'll discuss that with Mr. DeAngelo and get right back to you," Alexandra says before hanging up.

Someone above is definitely looking out for me. Carlo DeAngelo's long list of jobs will more than make up for any business Service Not Incidental steals, or so I hope. At least I know he will pay me well.

Adrenaline pumping, I return to my e-mails. That one call gets my creativity going, and now I am thinking up numerous promotions to keep and bring in customers.

While I am narrowing down those that can easily be implemented, the phone rings again. Maybe this is even better news.

"Hello."

"Roxanne?" A sexy baritone fills my ear.

"Yes?" I am sure I know who it is. No one else calls me Roxanne. But it has been months and I can't be sure.

"It's Max." Maxwell Porter is the hotel director on a popular cruise ship.

"What a nice surprise," I say, meaning it.

Max and I had been seeing each other off and on this summer whenever his ship was in town. Unfortunately, in the fall the cruise line had taken on a different itinerary and Max had pretty much disappeared. Not that that was unusual.

"I'm in New York until the holidays are over," he announces, sounding chipper, "Came in to be with my girl."

He couldn't possibly be talking about me. I hadn't seen him in months. I tried for flip.

"Sounds serious. Don't tell me love has finally struck the elusive Max. Who is she?"

His deep-throated chuckle warmed my heart. "You're my girl, silly."

I wanted to ask "since when" but didn't. I might be his New York girl but I strongly suspect Max has a woman in each port. Ours has always been a sexual relationship and we've lived in the moment. I know enough about Max not to have any expectations. He is charming and says all the right things, but don't ever expect a commitment.

Max is tall and resembles Shemar Moore. He can also charm the pants off the most devout woman. When you're with him you think you are all that matters, and when you're not, count on it, some other woman has his attention. But at least you can be assured a good time. Max spends money freely and seems to have plenty of it.

"I want to see you," Max insists. "How about you and me having dinner and then going dancing? There's a new restaurant on the Upper East I'd like to try."

"Where are you staying?" I ask. I already know this is a bed invitation.

"The Hyatt, midtown."

That means Max expects me to come in to New York City. He senses my hesitation because then he says, "I'll send a limo for you. Does seven o'clock sound good?"

I have no plans this evening and could use a night on the town. And I don't mind riding in style. Max is easy to be with and there is no mystery as to how the evening will end. There will be no false expectations beyond getting together the next time he's in town. That works for both of us.

"So what do you say, Roxanne?" he prods.

"I'll be ready at seven."

"Good. Wear something slinky and sexy. I've got gifts for you," he tempts.

Max always comes bearing presents. It's part of his makeup. Usually it is lingerie from some exotic part of the world. He has this thing for lace tap pants and skimpy thongs. And he's been known to throw in a French maid's uniform for good measure.

I hang up thinking this is good. I really need my ego

stroked and my engine revved. What I need even more is the mind-blowing sex that he can provide.

I need to focus and return to the business at hand. I've spent four years building a company I can be proud of and I'm not about to let two upstarts move in on my territory. Nor will I allow them to steal my customers. Desperate times call for desperate measures. I will pull out all the stops if I have to.

The holiday season provides lots of opportunity. I can come up with a unique gift for my customers if I have to; something they wouldn't ordinarily buy for themselves. I must go one better than the free service the competition is offering. Maybe if I offer a service guarantee; one hundred percent of your money back if not fully satisfied—that might do it.

Yes, it's risky and I am opening myself to every scam artist in town and some. But it is worth a try, and if I throw in an additional bonus, then I will keep my existing customers happy and pick up a few new ones, as well.

I begin typing, adding thoughts no sooner than they pop into my head. Nothing is too bizarre or outrageous to be dismissed. I am starting to feel pretty good about things when the phone rings again.

"Ms. Ingram?"

"Yes, Alexandra."

I recognize X's assistant's voice right off. She has the same slightly accented tones as he has. It speaks of foreign shores and sultry, romantic nights.

"Mr. DeAngelo is pleased you will consider caring for Bacci in your home," Alexandra says.

"Great. How old is the cat?"

"She is, we think, maybe fifteen." Alexandra fills me in on the cat's likes and dislikes. "There is one condition," she adds.

I hold my breath, waiting.

"Mr. DeAngelo wants to see where Bacci will be living. I'll need your address. Your home address, not your PO box."

My tongue practically trips me up when I give Alexandra the details. Carlo DeAngelo is coming to Malverne to see me? Things will never be the same. He will walk into my little Tudor house and look around. I need to call my cleaning service right away. The dust bunnies under those beds need to disappear.

Beds. My mind has already taken a quantum leap. We are already sharing one together. He and I are snuggling.

"What day did Mr. DeAngelo plan on visiting?" I ask. An image of me and Carlo tangled in satin sheets dances in my head.

"I'll check his schedule and get back to you." Alexandra hangs up.

I am still dazed. I wonder why Carlo has not delegated the property inspection to her. I'd think he had better things to do than to come out to Malverne unless...maybe it's me he really wants to see.

So far two nice things have happened today. Max is in town and out of the blue Carlo is coming to visit me. Things really are looking up.

A plan for a marketing promotion now takes root in my head, but it might mean hiring a graphic designer. If I sent out e-cards to my preferred customer base this might drive business. With a little bit of luck I can acquire new customers and at the same time one-up Service Not Incidental. By hook or by crook I am going to come out ahead.

I take a break to check on Vance and Lydia. Satisfied there are no issues that can't wait until tomorrow, I decide a manicure, pedicure and wax will be my treat. If I have time afterward I'll stop by Roosevelt Field Mall again and buy a new outfit. Comfort shopping.

Thinking of my child, I sober immediately. After Christmas, Lindsay is off to Paris and I already miss her. Some people eat their heartbreak away, not me, I've always shopped.

Later that evening and another session of retail therapy, I dress in my brand-new fitted black skirt with a broad belt cinching my waist. I'm wearing a champagne silk top and a cashmere shawl draped over the shoulders. I've used a sparkly pin to pull the whole thing together. And I am tapping my foot impatiently waiting for the limousine to pull up.

Like magic, a gigantic black Hummer slides to the curb; a Hummer limousine at that. The blinds at the neighbors' windows shift. They're a nosy bunch and nosier now that I am single. The minute I walk out my front door every phone line will light up. They'll be speculating I have a new man and a wealthy one at that. They get a kick embellishing what they don't know.

I put on my coat, grab my purse and hop into the back of the limo. I decline the wine the driver offers me and sink into the comfortable leather seats. I close my eyes and consider taking a nap. Max Porter will require all of my energy later.

"Miss Ingram. We're here."

The chauffeur's voice barely penetrates my haze. A hand on my shoulder gently shakes me awake.

"Mr. Porter's waiting inside at the table."

I have no recollection of how we've gotten into the city. I give my hand to the driver and step out onto the sidewalk. Using the other, I rummage through my purse.

"The gratuity has been taken care of, Ms. Ingram,"

says the bald driver with the midnight skin who reminds me of Michael Jordan. He leaves me under a striped awning and is back behind the steering wheel before I can protest.

I mince toward the smoked-glass doors of the restaurant. The same boots I wore to speed dating are beginning to pinch. The door opens before I can reach for the brass knob.

A ramrod-straight maître d' greets me. "Do you have reservations, madam?"

While he waits for my answer he positions himself behind the podium and peers into a book. A Tiffany lamp casts a golden glow over his face.

"I'm the guest of Maxwell Porter," I say.

I know Max is already here. He's always on time and if I know him he would have made reservations.

Predictably the maître d' says, "Mr. Porter is already seated. May I check your coat, ma'am."

"Certainly."

I leave my coat with the coat-check person and am whisked upstairs to a velvet upholstered banquette. Max is already working his way through a bottle of wine. Good wine, of course.

"Roxanne," he says, standing.

He is impeccably dressed as always. He kisses me on the lips, and that kiss leaves even my toes tingling.

"Just look at you, girl," Max says, twirling me around. "Girl, you are hot."

The $450 I've plunked out for my outfit is worth every dollar. Not that it will be on long, anyway.

Seated in the banquette I say, "It's good to see you, Max. You're looking good yourself."

Max is one of those buff elegant men that wears a T-shirt well but looks best in a tuxedo. Tonight, a navy suit sets off his caramel-colored skin to perfection. He has thick curly hair and hazel eyes that are sometimes hidden behind dark glasses. When he smiles, two dimples appear.

He reaches across the table and takes my hand. I am his.

"Miss me?" he asks.

"Of course I miss you."

I always miss Max. He is an easy person to be around and he is bright and engaging. I can talk to him for hours about anything. But I also know Max is one of those elusive types who hates being tied down. I knew that from the moment I met him on a cruise right after my divorce. What he did for me during that week, no psychologist ever could. And I will always be eternally grateful to him.

Max pours me a glass of the red wine he is drinking. The waiter hands us menus.

"You really look wonderful," Max says, after we've both made our choices. "What's keeping you looking so fine?"

"Hard work. Angst." I explain about Service Not Incidental and the ungrateful ex-employees. I omit mention of X and his being my savior. He is not a topic Max needs to know about. I tell him about Lindsay leaving for Paris and about my plans for the holidays.

Max tells me about his travels. I hang on his every word, enthralled by tales of exotic places.

"You can beat those two at their own game," Max says when the appetizer is served. "You're smart and savvy."

"Thanks."

He talks about the change in the ship's itinerary and how the Mexican Riviera is a change from the Caribbean. He tells me he is getting burned out and looking for a job on land. I am thinking he is stringing me along.

Duck, wild rice and asparagus tips are on my plate, salmon on his. He always did eat healthily.

The tip of Max's shoe nudges my ankle. We are playing footsie. The mating ritual has begun.

"You are spending the night." It is a statement.

Because I've anticipated something like this, I've stuffed a clean pair of undies and toiletries into my purse.

"I can."

"Good. We have a limo driver at our disposal so we can go anyplace that you want."

He manages to wedge a muscular thigh between mine. I am already flustered. Flustered and consumed by warmth. The red wine has nothing to do with the heat in my cheeks or me suddenly feeling dizzy.

"What's the plan? Are we still going dancing?" I ask. We've already passed on dessert, and the espresso and latte before us are getting cold.

"Your choice," Max answers, throwing it firmly back into my court.

Dancing, though tempting, is only going to prolong the inevitable. I am just as horny as he is. It has been months since we've been together and Max's citrus cologne is drawing me in.

"I am a little tired," I admit, smothering a yawn. "Why don't we just head back to your hotel?"

"Okay. We're out of here."

Max signals for the check and slaps down a credit card. He whisks me out of the banquette before the ink on that credit card slip is dry.

In the backseat of the Hummer I lay my head on his shoulder and let Alicia Keyes soothe me. He hums along while nibbling on my ear.

And then the most absurd thing happens. I see

Carlo's face clearly. It is him I am seated next to, it his teeth nibbling my earlobe and it his accented voice whispering in my ear.

I let the fantasies take over. Tonight I'll be making love to Carlo and not Max.

CHAPTER 8

In less than an hour we are at it.

"You're the best, baby. The best," Max grunts, as his thrusts increase and I writhe under him.

I dig my nails into his back and quickly slip over the edge.

"Yes!"

What seems an eternity later, Max stirs under me. "Gotta go to the bathroom, babe."

He leaves to take care of business and I curl into a ball, nude and satisfied. He has always been a phenomenal lover. Good sex is exactly what I needed tonight.

When Max comes back I wash up and then slide back under the covers. We make love again. I fall asleep knowing that I've been well taken care of in every area.

Next morning we have another leisurely romp and share a breakfast tray. Max gives me my gifts which are a sexy pair of red thong panties that play "Jingle Bells" and a set of black silk lounge pajamas with diamond cut-outs on the side. I model them for him and we make love again. Then it is time to leave. He walks me out to the Hummer and we make plans to see each other soon.

Time to return to the real world. I turn my cell phone on again. There are a number of messages waiting. Vance can't find the keys where a client said he's left them, and the poodle he is expected to walk is stuck inside whining. Hopefully Vance has called the client's emergency number.

Margot is on the verge of hysteria and needs to talk. Earl isn't returning her phone calls. Who can blame him? Another client needs me yesterday. His tenant is having plumbing problems and he is out of the country. I need to take care of the situation. That at least is an easy fix, I can call a plumber.

The graphic designer I'd left a message for has finally returned my call. He's excited about designing a singing greeting card and anxious to go to work. I return the call, discuss colors, copy, pricing and tell him just to be creative.

There are messages from potential clients inquiring about my services. These are good calls. I'll get back to them later. Then I hear my baby's voice and I come instantly alert. This child I live for.

"Plans have changed," Lindsay says. "I'm leaving for Paris as soon as school's out. I'm not going to be able to spend the Christmas holiday with you, sorry, Mom. Call me."

I am counting on Lindsay to be there with me. She is my family, the only relative I have in New York. My mother is remarried and lives in California with her new husband. My father abandoned us a long time ago. And you wonder why I have trust issues?

I now hit the redial button. The phone just rings and rings. Lindsay better be in class, but then why didn't she turn her phone off? I want to kill that child. I need her to get through the holidays. It is a depressing time for single people.

All the way back to Malverne, I think about why Lindsay wants to leave for Paris so soon. The ride from Manhattan goes quickly, with me getting more morose the closer we get. We are going against traffic so there is little stop-and-go. Soon, I am home.

I've enjoyed my evening out and needed it, but coming home is good. There's nothing like having your own bathroom and space. I've always thought that was another reason why relationships fail.

I wish the limo driver an early Merry Christmas and he takes off. I wander up the walkway, fumbling through my purse looking for my key. When I look up, I notice my front door is slightly ajar. Does that mean Lindsay has driven down from Skidmore to talk to me in person? That child is so impulsive and can be careless at times.

"Lindsay?" I call, sticking my head through the open doorway.

What I see inside brings me to my knees. It is pure destruction. My heart pounds and my breakfast lurches in my stomach. My house has been vandalized. I've been violated. The pillows from my sectional couch are strewn on the floor. Drawers from my sideboard have been emptied and items thrown on the carpeting.

I have an alarm system. I pay for monthly monitoring. Why haven't I gotten a phone call to alert me my alarm went off? Because I shut off my phone after retrieving some of my messages. Lindsay's message had thrown me for a loop and I'd prematurely exited voice mail.

What if whoever has looted my house is still here? I slam the door shut and race down the walkway. I find my cell phone and punch in 9-1-1. While I wait for the call to be picked up, I squat down on the sidewalk and place my head between my knees. I take deep, calming breaths and wait for the earth beneath me to stop quivering.

"Ms. Ingram are you okay?" a young voice asks.

I look up to find my neighbor's daughter, Jessica, looking down at me. Jessica is the precocious child who seems to spend most of her life outdoors. I sometimes wonder if she has a mother.

"No, I'm not okay, Jessica," I say, pulling myself together. "My house was just broken into."

Sirens are somewhere in the vicinity. A few seconds later, a police cruiser pulls up in front of my house. Two officers leap from the car and lumber up the walkway completely ignoring me as if I don't exist.

"I'm the sole owner of this home," I say, trailing them. "I called you."

Both men swing around and practically gaped. I am used to this reaction. Mixed neighborhood or not, people are still surprised to find a black woman home owner with a Tudor the size of mine.

"Roxanne Ingram," I say, introducing myself. I am feeling a little better. "I came home to find my front door open and my *home* ransacked." I emphasize the word *home* to make sure they understand I am the owner.

"Do you have a driver's license, ma'am?" The cop who looks like Fred Flintstone asks.

I find my license and hand it to him, wondering whether if I were white would I be asked to prove my identity. I also wave my house key at him.

His partner takes my key from me. They enter my house, hands on their holsters.

"Police!" they shout.

By now half of the neighborhood, meaning everyone without a day job, is gathered on my front lawn, Jessica's mom included. I field questions as best as I can. Nothing like this has happened in our immediate neighborhood before, and there is speculation.

"Could be someone you know?"

"Do you have a cleaning lady?"

"What about the handyman you used to fix your shed?"

Nothing passes by these people.

"The monitoring company didn't call you?" another neighbor asks.

"What did they take?"

And so it went on.

Finally the officers come back outside and assure me there are no further surprises inside, meaning no one is hiding. When I accompany them back in, tears finally begin to spill. Who would do this to me?

"We'll do a walk-through and you can determine if anything is missing," one of the cops says.

I lead both men through my ransacked home. All the major appliances and electronics are still intact. My television and entertainment center are where I left them and my microwave and other smaller appliances are still on the kitchen counter. The robber or robbers were clearly looking for money.

I remember the small amount of cash I keep on hand for emergencies and the jewelry left out in full sight. I rush into my bedroom to check. It feels like an icebox. The old metal box hidden under the laundry in my walk-in closet is open on my bed and empty. The money is gone.

The diamond studs I've left on the nightstand are missing and so is my tennis bracelet. The window above my bed is open, the curtain fluttering in the chilly winter air. That's where they made their escape.

"Whoever it is came in or left through that window." Flintstone's partner states the obvious. "There aren't any visible signs of forced entry. How many people have your key?"

"About three."

The cleaning service has my key and so do Margot and Lindsay. I keep an extra key hanging on the wall in the shed. I tell the police that.

"The detectives will come by shortly. They'll question anyone who has your key," Flintstone, who by now has introduced himself as Officer O'Ryan, says. "I'm going to check out the shed where you keep your extra key."

He leaves.

Head in my hands, I sink onto my bed. I am fighting back waves of nausea and I can't think straight. How has this happened?

"Is there someone you can call to be with you?" O'Ryan's partner asks. "The detectives should be here soon."

I don't want to be alone, nor do I plan to spend tonight in a house that has been broken into. I don't feel safe. I find my cell phone and speed dial Margot.

"You're back," she says gaily. "How did it go?"

I take a deep breath and steady my voice. "I came home to trouble," I say.

"What kind of trouble?"

I hear the panic in her voice but I am panicking myself and not in a position to calm either of us down.

"My home's been broken into."

"I'll be right over."

Margot is at my front door in less than ten minutes. By then, I am seated at my kitchen table, sipping on bottled water while the detectives, a man and a woman, dust for fingerprints.

O'Ryan returns to announce the key to my shed is missing. Margot asks him if there have been thefts n the surrounding towns.

He nods his head. "A couple. Kids. Gangs."

That is not very reassuring.

"And this has been going on for how long?" Margot asks, taking over. I am amazed that she is not hysterical. At times Margot surprises me.

"We've had a few reports of break-ins in the last two weeks or so."

Two hours later the police and the detectives finally leave. Margot insists on putting me to bed, then she sets about putting things right.

Later we call a locksmith and have the locks changed. I leave with her and promptly fall asleep at her place. I am exhausted and my emotions are way out of control. I have cried more than I ever have. Later that afternoon Margot drives me home.

I take a hot shower and dress in comfortable sweats. I've had my pity-party and now it's time to take back the reins. Margot hands me a long list of messages she's retrieved from my answering machine.

"You need to return these calls," she says.

I am still in that foggy stage of disbelief and glance disinterestedly at the paper. Some guy I've gone out with once and haven't given a second thought to has called. If I recall, he was duller than dishwasher and twenty years older than the photo he posted. This is fairly typical. Most men who post a profile are living in a fantasy world.

I sip on coffee and think about my missing cash and the jewelry I will replace. The irreplaceable pieces are gifts from my ex. Men today just aren't that generous, you're lucky if you're taken out to dinner and aren't left holding the check.

"I'm sure the cops are right about the thieves being kids," Margot says. "They grabbed what they could carry and left. They were looking for easy money."

"Probably."

I glance at the note Margot handed me. Lindsay still has not called. I need to hear from that child. She is beginning to worry me.

I speed dial her number.

"Yes, Ma," Lindsay answers.

When I hear her voice I forgive her everything. "What's this about you leaving for Paris before the Christmas holiday, baby?" I ask.

"Can we not talk about this right now. I have a class to get to in ten minutes," her voice is a plaintive wail.

"I want to talk about it."

The cell phone is snatched from my hand, and Margot speaks into it.

"Listen child, your house was just broken into and a bunch of stuff stolen. We're still not over the shock."

Margot shakes her head slightly. "No, I don't think it's necessary for you to come home." She turns to me. "You want her home?"

"Give me back that phone," I snap.

I arm wrestle Margot to get my cell back.

"So why do you have to leave for Paris before the Christmas holidays?" I ask Lindsay.

"Because I got my first runway modeling job, Mom. My agent needs me to be in Paris the week before Christmas. I'll be home next week. We'll celebrate early and I'll talk to you then."

I didn't even know the child has an agent. No, I will not make her feel guilty. She deserves to go to Paris and see if she has what it takes.

"Okay, we'll do Christmas next week when you come home. Love you, baby."

Tears flooding my eyes, I hang up. Margot's arms are open. Although it leaves me breathless I appreciate the hug. She is turning out to be a rock.

"It'll be all right, Roxi," she coos.

"It has to be." I sniff into her shoulder.

Cutting the apron strings hurt like hell, but Lindsay needs to find her own place in the world.

My motherly instincts are to protect her.

CHAPTER 9

The female detective, Hernandez, calls midafternoon with more bad news. There have been three break-ins in the surrounding neighborhoods last evening. No arrests have been made so far.

"This is scary," I say. "This used to be a safe town, where kids played outdoors without worries."

"We'll catch them."

She sounds confident. Sure. I wish I felt the same.

I've already written off any hope of recovering my money or the diamond jewelry that has been taken. And I've chewed out the alarm service for not calling me. They confirmed what I already suspected: the alarm wasn't turned on.

They might be right. I'd bolted from the house and hopped into that Hummer. I'd been in that much of a rush.

Even though I'm nervous about the possibility of another break-in, I am glad to be home and alone. Margot is only a phone call away, and in the harsh light of day things don't seem as bad.

I've already e-mailed my employees to postpone our weekly meeting. I check my calendar and realize with horror that tomorrow is the day Carlo DeAngelo is to stop by my place. The sensible part of me wants to cancel, the irrational other can't wait to see him. Max still hasn't called. I find that strange. I'll call him later to see what is up with him.

There are a couple of fires that need putting out. I call the customers and smooth them over. I take care of online banking for another and make arrangements at a ski resort for a wealthy family living on the North Shore of Long Island.

It is almost two full days since I check my personal e-mail and I am suffering from withdrawal. Two days is a long time for me, especially when I'm Internet dating. Who knows what I might be missing?

I enter the password for the e-mail I've created exactly for this purpose. I have ten messages waiting. Absence makes the heart grow fonder, I'm in demand.

After logging on to the site, I check the photos and profiles, ticking off in my head which ones to answer and which to ignore. I'm a big profile reader. Words tell you a lot. There's something about the way that some people phrase things that gives you insight into their personality.

Most as usual aren't worth the time of day. I sort

through the serial daters, easily identifiable by the form letters that are designed to impress. There are those looking for a quick hit, no strings attached. And there are the self-proclaimed studs surfing for people who've just joined. They've got the Internet rhetoric down pat:

"R u my angel."

"Wow! U r hot. Message me."

"I thought I died and went to heaven...cuz u r fine."

Enough already.

I scan another e-mail from a man who claims to be thirty-four and looking to get married. Judging by the accompanying photo, he's trimmed at least ten years off his age. I delete another with glaring misspellings, scan a few more and am finally down to my last e-mail. As I open this one I do my best not to get depressed. I'm getting to that point where I've pretty much given up on finding a match. The holiday blues are setting in.

There is no attachment, which means no accompanying photo. This is another red flag for me. When there is no photo I usually assume he is married or has something to hide. What keeps me reading is the message itself. He calls himself "Delicious," and I wonder if that's a sexual come-on.

I save the message in a folder to think about later and go off to call Max.

"What do you mean he checked out?" I ask the poor operator who'd placed me on hold for an eternity.

"There is no one registered by the name of Max Porter, ma'am," she answers with an edge to her voice that tells me I am on her last nerve.

I can feel the frown lines on my face deepen. Max is a free spirit. But we've made plans for the holidays, and disappearing without telling me where he's going is just plain rude. I expect better from him.

No expectations, Roxi. No expectations. Not when it comes to Max, anyway. Here today, gone tomorrow. But he's never been hurtful or a game player before.

"Mr. Porter didn't leave a forwarding address?" I ask.

"No, ma'am. He didn't."

Maybe Max has checked into another hotel and will call me later.

I hang up and try laughing it off. The truth is that with Lindsay preparing to leave the country, I am depending on Max to get me through the season. Max does everything with such style that it will be a pleasure to spend this difficult time with him.

No, I am not going to get depressed. I dig up the detective, Jolie Hernandez's business card and call her again.

"This is Roxi Ingram," I say when she answers. "I forgot to ask if you're increasing the number of patrol cars in my neighborhood."

"Yes, we plan to, ma'am. There'll be a man on your block every twenty minutes or so. Anything else?"

Jolie sounds harried and overworked so I hang up. This is the second time I've been called ma'am in the space of an hour. I am beginning to feel ancient. And my birthday is coming up in less than a month. Soon the dreaded four-O will hit me square in the face.

I glance at my watch. The cleaning service should have been here at least an hour ago. Margot has done a great job of putting the house back in order, but I am paying these people to clean. Really clean. I can't have Carlo in if there are dust bunnies under the bed and cobwebs in the corner.

No one picks up at the service so I leave a voice mail. I am pissed. I give these people plenty of business. I use them to clean my clients' houses, so you'd think they'd cut me a break. I should have first priority and at the very least a courtesy call. I am removing them from my list of preferred vendors. And finally I call Alexandra to confirm that Carlo is coming to check out the place.

"I haven't heard anything different," she says. "I can't interrupt Mr. DeAngelo. He's in a business meeting but if he has to cancel I'll let you know."

That's all I can ask.

"What kind of creations does DeAngelo create?" I ask before disconnecting.

"Memories. Our company specializes in experiences."

What the hell does that mean? Are they in the adult entertainment business? I've already stepped outside the boundaries of professionalism so better not push.

"I've got to go. The other line is ringing," Alexandra says, and quickly hangs up.

Since it looks as if the cleaning service is a no-show, I begin cleaning myself, something I hate to do. On the bright side, ninety dollars in my pocket is better than ninety dollars in theirs.

Four hours later I am done. Things look good from the surface anyway. It is pitch-dark outside and I start getting that queasy feeling in my stomach again. I check to make sure the windows and doors are all locked. Then I check the closets and under the bed. Convinced that there is no bogeyman hiding, I straighten things I've straightened before.

I settle on the couch to watch TV when Margot calls. She wants to know if I want to go for a drink at the neighborhood bar.

"Sure. Who's getting who?" I ask.

"I'll get you."

"Okay."

I agree primarily because I really don't want to be at home alone at night.

An hour later we pull into the parking lot of Island Breeze, the local tavern. What Margot forgets to tell me is it's "Hotties Night," the updated version of "Ladies night," and the place is jumping.

From the moment we swing through the front door we face a solid wall of men. Most are middle-aged and clearly in love with themselves, but peppered throughout are a few in their thirties. The stance is familiar, hip on the bar, eye on the door, beer in hand.

I groan loudly. Margot elbows me in the side. "Behave. It's a game. Just go with the flow."

Why have I allowed her to drag me here?

I paste a smile on my face and try not to bristle as I am being sized up. Margot sails me past a bunch of drooling men and we find a wall to lean on.

"I can use a drink," she says. "Can't you? And I'm not planning on paying for it, either."

With that Margot hands me her coat and hustles off.

Both of us can well afford to buy our own drinks so why does she feel it necessary to get some guy to pay. I don't want to have to chat some guy up because he's plopped down a couple of bucks for my drink.

I watch her head for the bar, hips swaying, booty bouncing. Like a dog on a bone, three men follow behind her. By the time she stops they are practically on top of her.

I hang up our coats on a peg on the wall and stand, my arms folded across my chest in a protective gesture. Someone once told me it signals that you are not open to conversation. I am not. I wonder what the hell I am doing here. I want to go home.

"Things can't possibly be that bad," a male voice says from behind me.

I turn to find a man of medium build, dressed conservatively in a jacket and tie, looking at me with a smile that indicates he finds me amusing.

"I'm not particularly fond of bars," I growl, intentionally sounding grouchy.

"Then why are you here?"

Good question. Honesty is probably the best policy in my case.

"My friend dragged me here."

"Would your friend be the petite woman surrounded by those men on the make?"

He angles his head in the direction of the bar. Sure enough Margot has acquired a string of admirers. It must have something to do with the ridiculously short leather skirt she'd insisted on wearing.

"That would be her."

We watch her navigate her way around the crowd, followed by two men carrying our drinks. I assume that she is bringing one of those men back for me.

"Pretend you and I are hooked up," I plead with the stranger.

"I'll go one better." He puts an arm around my shoulders and brings me close to him. He lowers his voice and tells me about his day, acting as if he and I are already planning our great escape.

"You move fast," Margot hisses in my ear when she arrives. "Now what am I supposed to do with this guy?" She hands me my drink. "Thank Dwight who's behind me for your drink."

I shrug. Not that I'm ungrateful, but Margot has taken it upon herself to pick up Dwight for me, let her handle it.

So there we are, two women and three men, shouting over the music and doing "bar speak."

The guy Margot has her mitts on seems nice enough. She is doing her helpless-little-girl routine and he is eating it up. Mine—the one I don't want—seems overly impressed with himself. He informed me almost immediately that he is a mortgage banker with a home on the north shore.

"Let's step out and get some air?" my newly acquired man suggests.

Excusing myself, I follow him out.

We stand on the sidewalk awkwardly.

"Out here I can breathe," he says, handing me

his business card. "I'm Josh by the way. Joshua Calloway."

"I'm Roxi." I fumble through my purse, find my card and tuck it into his open palm. We continue to face each other inhaling the chilly evening air.

"Think there'll be snow for Christmas?" he asks when we seem to run out of things to say.

"I'm hoping. I like a white Christmas."

Mundane conversation, but expected between strangers. At that precise moment I make up my mind to spend the holidays anyplace but New York. There is nothing to keep me here anymore. Max has fallen off the face of the earth and I can't count on Margot. She'll find a man just to get her through this bleak holiday period.

Cold penetrates my bones. I shiver. I feel as if the world is closing in. In a short space of time I've dealt with a break-in, a man who's gone missing and a daughter who's decided to skip town. Tomorrow I have to face a man I have an irrational crush on. Talk about sensory overload.

"You're cold. I should have insisted you bring your coat," Josh says, rubbing my arms.

He seems sweet enough but right now I am off men. I just want to go home, crawl under the covers and feel sorry for myself.

Josh is trying to rub some warmth back into me.

"You look unhappy? Are you?" he asks.

I don't know him but he seems sensitive and intuitive, two qualities I never ever associate with men. Since he is a stranger and I probably will never see him again I feel comfortable unloading. It will be therapeutic if nothing else.

So I tell him about what I've gone through these last few days. And by the time I am through I am damn close to tears.

"You poor baby," Josh says. "Let's go inside. I'll buy you a drink."

I follow him back in where it is warm and I let him buy me that drink. I look around for Margot but I can't find her anywhere.

I am tired and depressed. I want to go home.

I will walk home. My house is in walking distance. And I will use that time to clear my head.

Bah humbug. I really do hate Christmas.

Next morning I experience that slightly hungover feeling that drinking on an empty stomach creates. I'd only had three drinks. But there is something about being in tight quarters with no fresh air and inhaling the stale smell of booze that lends itself to a pounding headache. I have one of those aches now—the kind that lurks at the temples.

I pop a couple of aspirins, wash them down with two cups of coffee and hop into a hot shower. Afterward I go in search of something to wear.

I need an outfit that is professional yet sexy. Carlo DeAngelo needs to know I am a woman. I settle on a pair of tailored wool slacks and a silk kimono top. I step into my high heeled ankle boots, twist my hair into a knot and add chandelier earrings. Then I do a walk through of my "decorated by Roxi" house.

Satisfied that things look neat and tidy I sit down at my desk and boot up my computer.

The graphic designer I've hired has sent me prototypes of three different holiday cards. One I hate instantly, the other I am so-so about and the third I just love. I shoot him off an e-mail giving him the go-ahead on the third which is a singing holiday card.

Then I divvy up all the pending jobs between Vance, Lydia and Paula, my temporary hire. I send them all individual e-mails with specific instructions. I also make sure they know that this week our standard meeting is on.

I glance at the wall clock realizing it is already mid-morning. Perhaps I have time to peek at my personal e-mails. There is still the matter of my unanswered mail to "Delicious." Is he trolling to get laid? The screen name has turned me off but I am curious about the sender.

I take a deep breath and type, *Send me a photo*. Not that I am shallow or anything but I want to see who I am e-mailing. And I don't want to waste time.

As I am shutting down my computer, the doorbell rings. I take a few seconds to center myself and then I go off to answer.

Carlo DeAngelo stands on the front steps, gloves in hand. I feel like a teenager.

"Ms. Ingram? You are a Ms., I presume?" What he's really asking is if I'm married.

He looks pointedly at my left hand. I am wearing a ring on my wedding finger.

"I'm Roxi," I answer. "Please come in." I stand aside.

Carlo enters. Before I close the door behind him I notice the black Saab parked at the curb. There is no chauffeur waiting. He's driven himself here.

"Nice place," he says, looking around carefully.

My Tudor suddenly feels small. Carlo's very masculine presence makes me feel dwarfed. A citruslike scent fills my nostrils.

"I'll give you the tour," I offer.

This is business and he is here for a purpose.

"That will not be necessary. I have seen enough."

I scrunch up my nose. The man has driven all the way from Manhattan, fighting traffic all the way, to take a quick look at my living room and foyer. I wave a hand, inviting him to sit on my sectional couch. He sits, one leg crossed over the other.

"Tell me about Bacci? What does she eat and how often? Does she like toys?"

Carlo frowns as if I have said something wrong. "Do you not have pets of your own, Roxanne? You strike me as a most compassionate woman."

"I feed a stray cat." I explain about Bo Jangles. "My lifestyle does not allow for an indoor pet. I am too busy taking care of other people's needs. I'm like the shoemaker who repairs others shoes but his are rundown."

Carlo throws his head back and laughs. His caramel-colored eyes sparkle. "This is not good."

The conversation is becoming much too personal for my liking. Time to shift back to business.

"How long will you need me to care for Bacci?" I ask.

"I am thinking two weeks. The college student who normally feeds her is going home to New Hampshire. So I am in a bind."

"Is she declawed?" I think to ask, thinking of my leather upholstery.

"Yes, I took care of that long ago."

I whoosh out a sigh of relief.

Carlo stands and holds out his hand. His grasp is warm and firm.

"I will make arrangements to have Bacci dropped off on the twenty-third," he says. "Is that good?" I nod. He has one hand on the doorknob when he calls over his shoulder. "You are a most beautiful woman Ms. Ingram. And you are an intelligent business person. I am most impressed with you."

I am openmouthed as he closes the door behind him.

CHAPTER 10

"Hey, girl, why you sound so sour?" Margot asks the moment I pick up the phone. "I'm calling to invite you to a party."

"Who's throwing it?"

My focus is on the monitor of my computer and my dwindling funds. Business is dropping off and the numbers are not where I need them to be. I am seriously getting worried.

Margot's sentences come out in gushes. I listen with one ear while trying to figure out what's going on. I've picked up a bunch of new clients, but that's still not enough. I'm losing old ones, steady ones. I make a mental note to do something to get their attention, maybe send my singing holiday card with a credit or discount inside; this is in addition to other offers. Retention equals profits.

I am obsessing so hard about the drop-off in business that my brain actually hurts. I've already sent off e-cards offering a sizable discount to those who've used the service more than once. And I've snail mailed holiday cards to each and every client. My fingers still cramp from signing those cards.

"You're not listening." Margot's voice intrudes.

"Yes, I am, you said something about losing your key."

Margot's laugher bubbles through the earpiece. "No, hon. I asked if you wanted to go to a lock-and-key party with me."

Despite the dismal figures flashing before my eyes and my aching head, my interest is piqued.

"What's a lock-and-key party?"

"Back in college it was called a social, except this is the grown-up version. People come with the express purpose of hooking up with a member of the opposite sex. It's at a really nice location in the city. The women are given locks and the men have the keys. The object is to meet and mingle until you find the person whose key fits your lock."

"Sounds slightly perverted to me." I chuckle.

"It's effective from what I hear."

"Sure."

Margot fills me in on the date and place. The party is scheduled for five days before Christmas. By then I definitely will need some cheering up and it sounds like a pretty good idea to me.

After I get off the phone, I pick up the receiver again,

this time calling my banker. I need to find out if my loan has come through. I am starting to think radio ads and maybe some strategically placed advertising in the better newspapers might be worth it.

By the time I hang up with my banker I am feeling better than I have in a long, long time. I have excellent credit and have been approved for much more than I asked. I am not going to let the competition get the better of me.

I go out back, hoping to share my good news with Bo Jangles but can't find the cat. I come back in and plop down at my desk again. In just four days my baby will be winging her way to Paris. The thought makes my heart ache, but now I've decided to look at it as a positive thing.

I've always encouraged Lindsay to set her sights high and go for her dreams. Whatever those dreams might be. Nothing ventured, nothing gained I've often said. That has been my motto in life. And I've practiced what I've preached, risking everything to set up this business. I left a good-paying management position and used my savings to establish a company that has been reasonably successful. Until now.

I need a diversion. I am not going to let myself get crazy. I check the mailbox I've set up expressly for getting e-mails from the dating site. "Delicious" has responded to my request for a photo. I decide I will save looking at his picture for last.

After I've scrolled through a number of prospects, I decide none are for me and I return to Delicious's mail. He's attached a few photos of himself and is not at all what I expect. Brother-boy looks like the poster boy for corporate America.

Delicious is dressed in a crisp white shirt and burgundy power tie, his suit jacket dangles from one finger. He looks both powerful and intimidating. His hair is close cropped and has silver threaded through it. His nostrils flare slightly and his smile reveals strong even teeth. He is a man who exudes confidence.

Why is he on a dating site? I wonder. He should not have a problem finding women. Then again the same could be said of me. I am reasonably attractive, successful, and I don't have self-esteem problems nor do I come with a slew of children.

Since I am not sure what I want to do about Delicious. I do what any reasonable woman does. I do nothing.

My doorbell makes that ding-dong sound and I quickly log off. I can't imagine who would be at my front step at this time other than someone looking to sell me something. Since we're talking Long Island here I am cautious. I put an eye to the peephole.

"Who is it?"

A flash of silver. Some kind of a badge.

"Detective Hernandez," the voice says. "I'm in the neighborhood and took the chance you might be home. I have an update for you."

I open the door and Jolie Hernandez stands there, cup of coffee in hand, looking petite and slightly bedraggled.

The detective wipes her feet on the front mat and walks past me.

"We caught the thieves," she says before I can ask her to sit down.

My chest immediately feels less heavy. "That's great news. It's probably too much to hope that my bracelet and earrings were found?"

She chuckles. "Already sold and probably for a couple of bucks. We're talking teenagers here, although two of them might be in their early twenties. We caught them last evening in the middle of breaking into someone's home."

I thank Jolie. And yes, hearing the news does make me feel better. I am still nervous at night, fearful to close my eyes. What if they come back?

After Detective Hernandez leaves, it occurs to me that maybe I need to do my own snooping. I'll take a drive and cruise by Service Not Incidental. I hop into my car and follow Margot's directions. I set off to find where the two ingrates have set up shop.

I have to give my competition credit where credit is due. My ex-employees have chosen an area on the border of Hempstead and Garden City. They've done their homework. Garden City is too ritzy an address, but Hempstead suggests regular people. And the border where they've set up shop is well maintained.

I slow down in front of a row of homes set back from the street and squint until I find the number. The Victorian; a rambling monstrosity seems out of place in that location. But it has been restored and freshly painted. It has a huge wraparound verandah that holds gigantic pots of poinsettias. Boughs of greenery and red velvet bows adorn the balustrades.

I am drooling with envy. I rack my brains, how can these two young women afford such expensive rent? It makes me wonder what the heck I am doing wrong. Maybe I shouldn't have used my own money and used the bank's all along. Things are about to change now. I am inspired.

As I idle by, feeling just a little bit envious, a Honda Civic pulls into the curb and a woman gets out. It is my employee Lydia; the fink.

I burn rubber getting out of there. I make a stop at the post office to pick up a client's mail, then call a florist to order flowers for a client's mistress and his wife. This happens so often that the florist has jotted down the colors and flowers each woman prefers and is careful not to screw up the order. Irritated and not knowing who I can trust, I battle rush-hour traffic and head back. I am still steaming.

Usually I love this time of year, but now the holiday decorations and the piped-in Christmas carols are starting to get to me. Why do I feel as if life is leaving me behind?

Determined to take my mind off my misery, I think about the lock-and-key party instead, and the outfit I will wear. Not that I am expecting much in the way of meeting men, but dressing up and going out will give me something to do, and maybe I won't miss my child as badly.

I decide I need an endorphin high. My normal remedy for that is to go to the gym.

I am on my way to work out my angst.

"I think the bitch is pregnant," Margot says when we are halfway into Manhattan.

It's a week later and we've decided to take the Long Island Railroad so as not to worry about drinking and driving.

"What bitch?" I ask, keeping my voice low. I have a pretty good idea who she means but several people are taking an interest in our conversation and now they are shooting us strange looks.

"Earl's live-in or whatever she is," Margot says, impatiently. "If he has another mouth to feed, that's bound to affect my alimony payments. What am I going to do?" The sentence ends in a wail. I wonder if she's taken her medication. She is in one of her low moods, and I've been listening to her complain from the time we met at the Long Island Railroad Station.

I glance over at her. Margot's voice carries. The guy seated across the way from us has been listening intently. It still amazes me that a woman as attractive as my friend has such low self-esteem and doesn't value herself. Margot has a degree from New York University. She is able to get a job if she wants to. She doesn't.

"Earl's mandated by the court to pay you. He's never stiffed you before."

"That bitch will do anything to make sure I'm cut off. She'll find some way to convince Earl that their baby should have all his money. Just you wait and see."

I think she is being paranoid but I keep my mouth shut. "You'll make yourself sick worrying about nothing," I say.

The issue here seems more to do with Earl having another child than the actual money. Of course, I don't say so. Money has always been important to Margot. It is how she defines herself, and although we seldom speak of it, it must have hurt her deeply when her children, Malek and Sienna, were taken from her.

When your ten- and twelve-year-old children are given to your ex and a woman he is living with, it has to be an awful blow. I can't imagine having limited contact with my child with visitation only if properly supervised. And now Sienna and Malek are about to have a sister or brother.

The train arrives at Penn Station and we go outside and flag down a cab.

Fifteen minutes and a lot of traffic later, Margot says to the taxi driver sharply, "Make a right. You've almost missed the entrance to the park."

She is referring to Central Park where the event is being held. The organizers of the lock-and-key party are out to make a big splash and the price of admission reflects that. The establishment they've chosen, Tavern on the Green, is a New York landmark, and at this time of year guaranteed to be festively decorated and packed with tourists. We've each had to cough up a hundred bucks.

The cabdriver navigates around the hansom cabs and finally pulls up in front of the restaurant. We pay him and follow a stream of chattering people. I haven't been here since last summer, when I'd met with a client. We'd sat in the outdoor garden sipping frothy concoctions and admiring the colorful Japanese lanterns and potted impatiens and trailing ferns.

Judging by the crush of people ahead of us this lock-and-key party is going to be huge.

"Are you okay, Margot?" I ask. She's been unusually quiet. I hope she is not in shock. When Margot is in one of her down moods that doesn't bode well.

"I shouldn't have come," Margot says.

I feel for her. To tell you the truth I don't feel that great myself. Here we are both very single a few days before Christmas with another year under our belts. I am still amazed that Max has disappeared into thin air. I've gotten used to him popping in and out of my life, still, he's never been one to make plans and then up and disappear. I am wondering if something terrible happened to him. Even that thought makes me sick.

By the time we get to the registration desk, it is almost three people deep. After what seems a considerable time we are able to get name badges and locks. We push and shove our way into the crowded restaurant with others there for the same purpose: meet, mingle and hope.

Inside has been converted into a twinkling winter wonderland. Amidst the greenery and boughs adorning the ceiling, sparkling angels fly. Potted mini Christmas trees sport real Christmas lilies and exotic ornaments hang. The smell of pine is everywhere, and set back in a corner a three-piece band plays holiday songs.

My mood perks up as I watch the crowd on the dance floor. People are determined to have a good time. Arms are in the air and hips are swaying. I smell beer. The group seems very young to me. What am I doing here?

"Come on," Margot says. "Let's circulate and check out the possibilities." She is on a high again.

I follow her through the crowd, an eye out for available seating. After a while I decide it's not in the cards and head for one of the bars with Margot trailing me.

It takes us almost twenty minutes to get drinks. We've had a few men approach with keys and in the spirit of things we've held out our locks. There's been no fit so far. The banter back and forth is quick, light and upbeat. But none of the men are what I have in mind. I want what the rest of the world wants—tall, dark, handsome and more than gainfully employed. I have a business to protect.

"Time to move on," Margot says, nudging me along with that determined gleam in her eye. I've gotten used to her rapid mood changes.

Lock held above her head, Margot whips her way through the crowd.

"Yo, yo, yo! Where you two fine ladies heading?"

A giant stands in our path, preventing us from moving forward. He has smooth dark-chocolate skin, a body that looks as if it was hewn out of stone and light gold eyes. It is the "Yo," that gets to me. It doesn't match his corporate attire.

But Margot is smiling up at him and holding out her lock. The giant quickly obliges by inserting his key. This has become a mating ritual.

"Think you and I might fit better?" he asks, winking at Margot and taking her arm. "Dr. Theodore Fitzpatrick. Theo to you. I'm a gynecologist."

Score one for Margot. They are growing doctors differently these days. This one, professional as he appears on the outside, definitely sounds like a homeboy.

Margot is already preening like a lapdog. The "doctor" before Theo's name will keep her at his side. He is probably as good as it is likely to get tonight.

I decide to move on and let them become acquainted.

Despite the cold temperature outside, it is starting to feel muggy. Too many people. Too much body heat. I find a spot in a corner where I can people watch and sip on my Bellini.

"I've got the key if you have the lock." A clipped male says from behind me.

Despite the cheesy line, I can't help smiling. I look

into a pair of eyes so dark they are almost black. My new friend is of average height and build and seems as uncomfortable about being here as I must look. But at least he is trying.

"So where's your lock?" he repeats, waving his key at me.

I reluctantly produce the lock I've hidden behind my back.

After inserting his key he shakes his head ruefully. "Jeez, no fit. How about we just agree that it fits." He winks at me. "It'll save you and me the painful process of having to work our way through this crowd. I'm Keith by the way."

"Roxi," I answer, clasping the hand he holds out.

"Roxi? Let me guess, short for Roxanne."

I nod.

"What say we get another drink, Roxi?"

Over my shoulder I hear, "Roxanne, who would think we'd run into each other here."

I don't place the voice initially but curiosity prompts me to turn around to see who it is.

"George Foster, remember me?"

I quickly scan my memory then it comes back. George is the restaurant owner I'd met online. Trying to get together had been a challenge. There'd always been some problem: broken cell phone, bad hard drive, meetings out of the country. Finally we'd done dinner. And, by George, my George had found the waitress's belly button ring more fascinating than my conversation.

Between courses he'd stuck a finger in the woman's navel and the two had forgotten I existed and begun flirting outrageously.

That as far as I was concerned was the end of the night.

I'd stormed out of the restaurant and he'd shouted after me. "Roxanne, baby, what have I done wrong?"

And now here he was standing, waiting for me to say something.

CHAPTER 11

"George, ah, George. Of course. I remember you." I manage a smile.

He bends over to kiss my cheek and I almost puke. Why am I making the effort to be gracious?

"We lost touch," he explains to Keith when he straightens up. "She's a wonderful girl."

I am nobody's girl, and this isn't exactly true. Right after the belly-button incident he'd called and I'd told him I never ever wanted to see him again, not in his lifetime or mine.

Keith, picking up on my discomfort, hooks an arm through mine.

"We're on our way to get a drink," he says breezily, dismissing George with a nod. I like this guy.

"Have fun. Merry Christmas," I say, shoving off.

I ignore George's frosty stare.

When I wrap my palm around another drink, I look around hoping to spot Margot. She's lost amidst the sea of eager young women looking for locksmith assistance.

After a few more minutes of uninterrupted conversation, Keith and I are approached by a group of men and women hoping to find a match. The conversation is lighthearted and easy, even silly, but we are laughing a lot. Some are on their way to inebriation and I'm starting to get depressed, which comes from knowing that no one here is going to make my heart go pitter-patter.

But people are starting to hook up. A few are already heading for the door and on to more-intimate locations. Others, figuring why wait, are already in lip locks. Keith is now talking to a full-figured light-skinned woman with a mane of hair. She is making no bones about letting him know she wouldn't mind taking him to bed.

I leave them to it. It is late. I am tired. And frankly I'm feeling down. The place is really beginning to empty out. The dance floor now holds only a few drunken swaying couples. There is still no sign of Margot and her self-proclaimed doctor.

I get out my cell phone and punch in her number. It rings forever. Right before voice mail kicks in Margot picks up. She sounds fuzzy, as if she's been drinking.

"Roxi, I swear, I've been trying to call you, I just couldn't get through."

Right!

"Where the hell are you?" I ask, skipping the niceties.

Wherever she is there is virtually no background noises which makes me suspect— Actually it is none of my business.

"Uh," she says—the woman's not stupid. "Theo and I left to get a drink. It was too noisy in there."

That can mean just about anything. For all I know she could already be at the doctor's place, and I strongly suspect she is.

"Listen," I say. "I'm done. I'm going to try to catch the 11:05p.m. train home."

Margot's voice is a murmur as she consults her doctor. She comes back on the phone to say, "Go ahead if you want, Theo will drive me later."

I bet he will. I hang up without saying another word. This isn't the first time, nor will it be the last time, she abandons me. Margot has her priorities.

I go out front where several cabs are lined up and I get into one.

"Penn Station," I tell the driver.

The Long Island Railroad I can count on, barring no strikes or breakdowns it will get me home.

Two days later, Bacci, Carlo's cat, gets dropped off by Alexandra. The feline weighs easily twenty pounds and immediately begins following me around the house. I soon get the feeling I'm being stalked. When she isn't roaming, sniffing and marking territory, she makes herself at home in my walk-in closet and takes to peeing on my shoes. Once I've sniffed out this problem I warn her that she'll become chop suey if she continues. I stuff her into the laundry room where there is tile and she can do minimal damage.

I've already said a tearful goodbye to Lindsay yesterday when she'd spent the night. We did some serious mother-and-daughter bonding, and I am slowly getting over what I consider her abandonment of me.

Margot, I haven't spoken to since the night of the lock-and-key party when she'd bailed on me. She's called several times but I haven't been in much of a mood to talk to her.

My landline rings now and I groan. Margot is relentless, a bulldozer at times. I'm resigned, might as well get the confrontation over with now, rather than push it off until later. It is the season to be charitable. I go off to answer.

"Okay, girl," I say, "I accept your apology."

"Roxi, this is Lydia."

I heave in a breath. I suspect I know what is coming next.

"You're calling to check on your schedule," I say, and wait.

A gigantic pause follows. "I'm calling to quit."

I feign surprise. "Why? I thought you were happy. Are you having personal problems? If so, we can work something out. You are planning on giving me two weeks' notice?"

"I'm sorry I can't." She sounds as if she is choking.

Despite my vow to remain calm, I lose it. "What do you mean, you can't give me two weeks notice? Is this a family emergency? Are you leaving the country? What?"

"I found another job," Lydia admits reluctantly. Now it's my turn to be silent. Let her squirm. "They're paying me a lot more money than you are," she wails. "Please try to understand. I need the money."

"Since when?"

Lydia is a rich girl from Connecticut. This college kid drives a BMW.

"Who is *they?*" I pry. "*They* wouldn't by chance be Karen Miller and Tamara Fisher?" When she doesn't answer right off, I go for the jugular. "I saw you coming out of Service Not Incidental's offices recently. Are they who you're going to work for?"

"They called me. I didn't go to them," Lydia blabbed.

I smell my ex-employee Kazoo behind this migration. Will Vance be next? "Fine," I snort. "So much for loyalty and for being decent." I can counter with more money but don't want to. I no longer trust her. I just want her gone.

"Try to understand. I really need the money," Lydia pleads. "My dad expects me to contribute to next semester's tuition. Karen and Tamara are offering me a salary plus commissions."

"I'll mail your check," I say, and slam the phone down. I am short on patience.

My business is slowly falling apart. And now I don't know who to trust. My best friend has abandoned me for some guy she picked up and my employees are dropping like flies. Vance will probably be the next to quit. I'm desperate. I need to do something quick.

Bacci meows behind me. She's escaped the laundry room again. I find some momentary comfort as I scratch the corpulent cat behind her ear. My thoughts then shift to her attractive owner. Is Carlo enjoying the holiday with an attractive woman? A man who looks like him must have several ladies on a string. I feel a rush of excitement as I think about him. It's a hopeless crush, and I doubt it will ever be requited.

"What am I going to do?" I say to Bacci, who is staring at me and rubbing her furry side against my leg. "This is my busiest season."

Because I know she can be counted on in a pinch, I give in and call Margot. She picks up on the first ring.

"Good, I'm finally off your shit list," she says. "What's up?"

I tell her that Lydia has quit.

"Why, that rotten little bitch. I hope you make her wait for her paycheck."

"I need you to fill in," I plead.

"You know I will. I'll just have to pop a couple of happy pills. Your customers will get the best service they've ever experienced."

"I can't thank you enough, girl," I lob back. "It's just until I hire someone. Christmas is a few days away, and I have a long list of people who need to be shopped for. Thank God you love to shop."

"Until I drop," she assures me.

As much as she sometimes frustrates me, Margot can be counted on to watch my back. It is one of the reasons I love her. When I really need her she is there.

The conversation shifts. She gives me the 4-1-1 on Doctor Theodore Fitzpatrick who she claims has more stamina than any man she knows. She goes on and on about him until I have had my fill. Too much information. I'll never be able to look the man in the eye again.

"You are the best," I say, ending the conversation. I'd like to hug her but she isn't here. "Come by tomorrow and I'll give you the job list and my corporate card. And, Margot, I want you to buy something special for yourself."

"You know I will, girl. I need something hot to wear to that Christmas dinner party. You are coming with me?"

I almost forgot. My gift is going to cost plenty.

Feeling a little better, I check on Vance. He assures me he is still with me and has no plans to leave.

"You gave me my first good paying job, if I'm not loyal to you, my mama will have my hide."

To keep him loyal I give him a huge raise and the promise of commissions on future jobs. He seems pleased.

I then call my new employee, Paula. When I identify myself she sounds a bit strange. I suspect that either Karen or Tamara has gotten to her. I do what any desperate woman would do given the circumstances. I resort to old-fashion guilting. I remind her that I'd hired her when she was in need. And then for good measure I give her a raise, too, and also dangle the promise of commissions in front of her. Hopefully that will be enough to keep her with me at least through the season.

After all this convincing I am burnt. I need something mindless and entertaining. What else is there to do but to log on?

I've gotten a few winks from guys who've posted their profiles but are too cheap to subscribe. They're commitmentphobes or just plain cheapskates I decide.

Delicious's name pops up, and I do a quick intake of breath. He is beginning to grow on me and I am concerned when I don't hear from him. But there is a consistency to his inconsistency. His e-mails so far have been bland but classy. He usually tells me what he's up to and inquires about how I am doing. He never probes or in any way crosses the line. I wonder what he really wants, since he never comes right out and says so. But he does give me his phone number this time.

I type back a few quick words and add my phone number. Max's total disappearance has left me wary. I've decided if you're interested in me then you need to put yourself out a bit. I'm not being overaccommodating.

My doorbell rings. I rise and put my eye to the peephole. I don't recognize the man, but he is burly.

"I've got something for Roxanne Ingram," he says.

I don't see an ID nor does he look like a postal worker. He is wearing a nondescript ski jacket and drab brown pants. It is the holiday season and he could be a con man, plus my house has recently been broken into.

I grab a broom. I'll use it as a weapon if I have to. I inch the door open and am handed a legal-size envelope.

"Have a good rest of the day, ma'am," the man says before I can close the door on him.

I take the envelope with me into the kitchen and pour myself a cup of tea. Then I get a knife and insert it under the flap. I withdraw an official-looking piece of paper.

When I glance at it I almost have a heart attack. I am being taken to small claims court by an upset parent who claims her toddler's clothing is ruined and her child's head messed up, and all on account of the drunken clown I'd hired to entertain at that party in Lawrence.

Ms. Betsy Nelson's child had been so upset she'd lost control of her bladder and ruined a three-hundred-dollar party dress, her undergarments and patent leather shoes. Since that unfortunate event, the Nelson child has become a bed wetter. In total, the Nelsons are suing me for two thousand dollars, which includes the price of the gift for the birthday boy and the psychologist's bill to date.

Someone up there is conspiring against me. If this streak of bad luck continues, I'll be needing a shrink.

I punch in the number for my attorney and wait for a secretary to pick up. While the phone rings on the other end I mumble a silent prayer.

"Please, God, let this be over with soon."

CHAPTER 12

Stephen Little is my attorney, although he is more friend than lawyer to me. He and I went to college together. Stephen and I reconnected when I first thought about incorporating my business. Now I rely on him for sound advice, especially when things threaten to become litigious.

"The claim about the Nelson child being traumatized is probably bogus," Stephen advises in his warm baritone. "I'd pay the Nelson woman the two thousand dollars and get it over with. It will buy you goodwill, plus you don't need the stress. Get her to sign a release, though. Who wants to go to small claims court over such a small sum of money?"

I agree with him. But now my expenses are building and my clients are dwindling. Two thousand dollars isn't chump change to me. Plus, I still have Christmas shopping to do. I gave Lindsay a sizable amount of money before she left. I have Margot to buy for and I have gourmet baskets to send to my corporate clients, and yes, they'll get there late.

My mother will get an IOU for the cruise I've promised her.

I'm not feeling guilty, because my mom wants for nothing. She's doing better than I am and she's got a man in her life who's supportive. I need to buy a hostess gift for Susan Watson, who's hosting the dinner party on Christmas Day that Margot got us invited to. And I need to make some kind of dish.

All Susan's guests are supposed to be single. We're a collection of never marrieds, empty nesters and those freshly out of divorces. The only reason I'm going along as Margot's "single" is because it will keep my mind off Lindsay and Max.

"Thanks for the advice and have a nice holiday," I say to Stephen, and ring off.

My phone jingles as soon as I disconnect. I don't recognize the number. "Wife for Hire."

"Roxanne Ingram, please."

"This is Roxi."

"Keith Santiago. We met at the lock-and-key party last week."

Knock me over with a feather. I wasn't expecting Keith to call. We'd exchanged numbers but I'd figured that was that.

"Of course I remember you, Keith."

We talk for several minutes and he invites me to have

a drink in the city the next time I'm in. I hang up feeling better. Someone still finds me attractive.

My doorbell rings and I put my eye to the peephole. I am not expecting anyone.

"Who is it?"

"Florist, ma'am."

"Hold up your ID please."

A square plastic badge gets held up to the peephole. Still, I open the door with caution. The deliveryman is holding a white poinsettia of gigantic proportions. It looks more like a tree. He shoves it at me.

"Someone loves you, hon," he says, as I stagger under the weight of the basket.

"Just a minute." I close the door with the tip of my shoe, set the plant on the coffee table and grab my purse.

I tip him and wish him Merry Christmas. He leaves whistling.

This is by far the best thing that's happened to me today. I remove the card nestled amongst the leaves and insert a nail under the flap. I'm trying not to get my hopes up. Maybe Dave has come to his senses. Maybe he realizes I am the best thing that has happened to him since pumpernickel, or maybe Max is repentant.

I hold the card and stare at it. My mouth flaps open then euphoria takes over. I soar. This is my dream come true.

Dear, Roxanne:

I hope I am not being too forward. This is to thank you for taking good care of Bacci. I hope you have a nice Christmas and a wonderful new year.

Best,

Carlo DeAngelo

I hold the card close to my heart and gulp air. I take long deep breaths, soothing breaths. Maybe I am reading too much into this. Carlo is only being polite.

I place the poinsettia on the floor in front of the unlit fireplace. It brightens my living room and puts me in a Christmassy mood. It inspires me to decorate; something I have not had time to do. I go off in search of the garlands and fake berries I have packed in boxes in the attic. Two hours later I am done. The place looks festive and I am on an adrenaline high. I hum carols to myself.

My phone begins to ring like crazy. I can barely keep up with the last-minute rush. People are panicked and feeling overwhelmed. This means money for me. I tell everyone who calls I can help them, though truthfully I am taking on more than I feel comfortable with. Somehow I will manage.

I call Margot and my standby crew; not the most

reliable bunch at times, but I need bodies. Some are available, and I assign them chores such as picking up deliveries, grocery shopping and tracking orders already placed.

I still need to do my own Christmas shopping, and some of it I do online, paying premium prices for on-time delivery. I break down and order a gourmet basket for my mother and her love. Then I leave to do my own grocery shopping.

Christmas Day comes. It is cold and drab outside. I am hoping for snow, not a lot of it, just so the sidewalks are coated in powder and I can say we had a white Christmas. I am not feeling myself and I try hard to shake the low feeling.

I move my poinsettia to the bay-window seat then I start a fire. As I am pouring coffee, my landline rings.

"Merry Christmas, Mom," Lindsay greets me. She sounds elated and her voice is as clear as a bell. It is as if she is right next door.

My heart leaps just hearing her voice, and my throat tightens up. But she sounds happy and I am happy because she is happy. Oh, to be young and carefree.

"Merry Christmas, hon," I answer with renewed enthusiasm. "What's good with you?"

She tells me about a modeling job she has landed

and the dinner she is on her way to. Paris is six hours ahead of us and Christmas is already half over with while ours has just begun.

I tell her about my own dinner plans, making sure to sound enthusiastic. Events like this one can so easily turn out to be depressing and I need something uplifting and fun. I glance at my beautiful poinsettia with the white and silver ribbons and get an immediate pick-me-up. How can I be down when Carlo is thinking of me?

"I love it over here, Mom," Lindsay enthuses, her voice holding wonder. "It's so me. You should think about visiting."

"I will," I say, meaning it. Paris has always been a dream on my list and I need a vacation. "How are the children?" I ask carefully, meaning the children she is being paid to take care of.

"Wonderful. They are sweet and bright. They make me want to have kids of my own."

My leaping heart stops. Lindsay is so young and so passionate. But kids? She is not ready. She reminds me of me a long time ago. Much as I love her don't want her repeating the same mistake. She does not need to be thinking of kids at nineteen.

"I'm glad you're enjoying yourself," I say.

"I am. And French is coming easily, Mom. I'm going to be fluent. I just know it."

I am glad she feels confident. All those years of French lessons will be worth it, then. We blow each other kisses and express our mutual love. After hanging up, I find the date bread I made last evening, nibble on it and sip coffee.

It's not quite midmorning yet, but I've already devoured two slices of bread and am considering breaking opening a box of truffles. My phone rings again.

"Merry Christmas," I say, without looking at caller ID.

"Merry Christmas, stranger. Do you know who this is?"

"Not a clue."

The male voice is deep and seductive. It gives me shivers. I like the sound of the man's voice so I wait.

He chuckles. Another shiver skitters up my spine.

"Don't keep me in suspense."

"It's Delicious," he supplies. "Thought I might touch base and see if Santa's been good to you."

He's been good to me now. My new Internet friend is the last person I expect to hear from. It is a very *delicious* surprise.

"How did you get my number?" I ask, then I remember I sent it to him.

He chuckles again. His laughter is deep and throaty and goose bumps pop out.

"You sent it in your last e to me," he reminds me gently. "Where in the city do you live?"

"I'm on the Island," I say carefully, "and you?"

"The City, though I'm heading for Mount Vernon to spend the day with my family."

Mount Vernon is in Westchester County, New York. It's where Denzel Washington grew up and it has a huge mostly black middle- to upper-middle-class population.

"Let's get together next week," Delicious suggests. "I'll call to firm things up."

We exchange real first names—his is Reed, and we chat as if we've known each other for ages before hanging up. Now I feel as if I've been given two very nice Christmas gifts and my mood picks up.

I go in search of Bacci. I feed her small pieces of the turkey I roasted last evening when I was in Suzy Homemaker mode. Because I'd felt energized and optimistic, I'd made an entire dinner and baked the date bread. If you're used to feeding a family, old habits are hard to break.

Bacci chows down, enjoying every last bite. She purrs and rubs against my ankles. I take my third cup of coffee into the living room and she joins me as I sit cross-legged in front of the fire. I open the few gifts I have received.

Lindsay's gift, the one she dropped off during her

overnight stay, makes my eyes water. It's a red cashmere shawl that I've had my eye on but was too cheap to buy. She's given me a trendy, sparkly broach to go with it.

My employees, what's left of them, bought me a pair of Coach gloves and a scarf that's also Coach. I feel guilty because they've been extremely generous. Then why is it I still don't entirely trust them?

My mother, who is leaving for wine country today, mailed her gift almost a week ago. It's a certificate for dinner for two at B. Smith's, the restaurant named after its elegant ex-flight-attendant owner. Mom's also sent me a pair of warm slippers. I wonder what she's trying to tell me.

The morning's almost over and I still have to shower. I've accomplished very little but I feel so much better. I take a hot shower and start getting dressed. My cell phone rings as I am buttoning up a festive red satin blouse. I pick up the phone and depress the button. "Merry Christmas," I sing.

"Hey, girl, Earl just called. Can you believe it?" Margot trills, sounding as if Santa has arrived with a sleigh filled with goodies. "He says he'll come by later."

"For what?" The question pops out before I can stop it. "I thought you guys had a no-contact order."

"Yes, but…"

I listen to her go on. I can already write this script. She and Earl will end up sleeping together.

"Are you canceling on me?" I ask.

"Heck, no, we're still going to dinner. I'm just not spending hours there."

"That's fine with me."

I'm glad we're still going. I need to keep busy. Sitting at home on Christmas Day is much too depressing, and I am in a good mood. After she tells me what time she'll come by to pick me up, we hang up.

It's turning out to be a good day after all.

Susan Watson's home in Northport is a mac-mansion. She's a real estate agent, selling million-dollar houses, and does well for herself. Cars are double-parked in the circular driveway and on both sides of the street when we arrive.

I juggle a bottle of champagne, a loaf of date bread and a handblown glass ornament for Susan's Christmas tree. I hope she likes my gift.

"How much do you think this house goes for?" I ask Margot as we climb the front steps. The railings are draped in fresh greens and berries, and laughter comes from inside.

"Close to two million. It was being foreclosed on and Susan got a good buy."

I've met Susan before but she might not remember me. She's sophisticated and articulate and so successful that if you're not confident she intimidates you. Susan is single and plans on staying that way.

Margot rings the doorbell. She is the epitome of chic today in her fur jacket, green ankle-length velvet skirt and high-heeled boots.

The front door is thrown open and Susan, a light-skinned African-American woman greets us. She appears bigger than life.

"Merry Christmas," she gushes, holding out a cheek for us to air kiss. "You two look fabulous."

As we make our way inside, a number of smells converge. There is that piney odor that shouts "holiday season," the mouthwatering aroma of duck and the smell of cranberries and baked goods. And there is more laughter. Glasses are clinking and voices are raised. Suddenly I am glad that I have chosen to spend Christmas surrounded by people.

"Let me introduce you around," Susan offers, after relieving us of the things we've brought. She sets them down on her already overburdened buffet table and takes Margot by the hand. I follow them into a spacious den overlooking Long Island Sound.

No one even notices our arrival because they're busy laughing at the antics of a heavyset woman, dressed to the nines in a burgundy velvet jacket and crisp white shirt with ruffles at the sleeves. I can tell she is used to being upfront and center.

She has auburn hair cropped close to her scalp. Her makeup is flawless, and she gesticulates with nails that are a work of art. Despite her size she moves with confidence.

Champagne is being poured by a balding man of indeterminate age. Susan has taken holiday decorating to the nth level. Rose-colored tulle frames the window walls and clusters of holly and ivy are used as accents. Fluttering silver doves and string instruments float from her ceiling.

In the corner is a monstrous Christmas tree. It is pink and silver and the hugest fairy I've ever seen graces the top.

Susan claps her hands to get everyone's attention.

"Hush for just one minute, y'all," she shouts. "I want you to meet Roxi and Margot."

Several pairs of eyes flicker over us. The women are checking out our makeup and outfits. The men are deciding whether we're worth more than a look. I smile. I wave. I hope I appear warm.

"So where's our champagne?" Margot asks.

A tall, classy-looking bald man hands us two flutes. Room is made for us on one of the comfortable couches. Another man comes by with a bottle and pours the champagne. He introduces himself.

"Hi, I'm Will."

Will is short, rotund and jovial. He works the room, stopping to chat with just about everyone. He and Veronica, the heavy woman, who's been holding court, exchange friendly jabs. Margot and I meet Stephen, a banker, who Margot begins to flirt outrageously with, Dr. Theo forgotten for the moment.

We meet Delores, who seems shy, and Tanisha who wears blond locks elegantly. There is Cora who is ultraglamorous and shouldn't have trouble finding a man. Yet she is here.

Susan leads us over to two men holding an animated conversation. We meet Mohammed and Tim. Both are nondescript but seem nice enough. Outside on the dock sucking on cancer sticks are a small group of smokers.

The first glass of champagne goes down easily. I feel even happier and more elated. I sample the pâté and shrimp cocktail served. I nibble dim sum.

The smokers come back inside. They call noisily for champagne. Cora is now quizzing me. She wants to know what I do. She wants to know where Margot got her outfit. Stephen, the banker who's been commandeered by Tanisha, excuses himself and returns to Margot's side.

Margot resumes flirting and I decide to circulate. I chat with several of the women, but I am drawn to Veronica, who, like me, runs her own business. We talk about what it's like managing a minority-owned business and trying to get our names out there.

Will interrupts us. I can tell he's attracted to me, but although he seems nice, it's not happening for me. Susan comes out of an inner room bringing a round little woman wearing a chef's cap with her.

"Dinner will be served shortly," she announces.

Will holds out his hands to us. Veronica and I escort him into the dining room.

It's turning out to be a very nice Christmas after all. I'm having a good time.

Now I can't help wondering what the new year will bring.

CHAPTER 13

It is the week after Christmas and everything comes to a grinding halt. There is virtually no business. When the phone rings I almost break my ankle getting to it.

"Is this Wife for Hire?" a querulous female voice inquires.

"Yes, this is the owner, Roxanne Ingram, is there something I can help you with?"

I wait, hoping that she has a long list of tasks that need doing. Wife for Hire could definitely use the business.

I am used to things slowing down after Christmas, but this year they seem slower than usual. I am hoping that things will pick up in a day or so. With New Year's Eve rapidly approaching maybe some people will plan last-minute dinner parties and need help.

I count on hectic lifestyles and general disorganization to keep me in business. I am counting on that now. My phones need to ring. I keep checking my e-mails for Internet business.

"Who is this?" I ask when the silence on the other end continues.

"Rona Saperstein." The woman heaves out a sigh. She sounds overwhelmed.

"I'm desperate," she admits. "And glad to find you open. My husband surprised the family with a ski trip to Vermont. I'll need someone to take care of my son's snake in our absence, and I'll need help with the mail and newspaper, plus I have plants that need watering. Can you handle it all?"

A snake! Yikes. My brain goes into overdrive. I hate reptiles. "How long will you be gone?" I ask carefully. I've had a few snakes before, but Kazoo was always the one who cared for them. He shopped for the food and fed them their diet of live mice. My stomach lurches at just the thought. With him gone I can't think of a soul to handle the feeding. But I'll find someone or die trying.

"Well, can you do it or not?" Rona Saperstein persists. Her whining voice would drive anyone crazy. She must sense my hesitation because now she becomes very manipulative. "Those people at Service Not Incidental didn't want to touch Eve. I offered them double the going rate and they still said no. They have that two-for-the-price-of-one special but they claim feeding a snake didn't qualify."

"SNI is providing two services for the price of one?" I repeat, despite my dry mouth and the whirring in my ear. These people are looking to put me under.

"Yes, that's what they say in their radio ads. I called, but no dice. I have to tell you I was not impressed with the way I was handled."

Radio ads? Jeeze, that's expensive. Where are these two women getting that kind of money? I need to do something or I'll be put out of business.

"I'll do it. I'll take care of Eve, the mail, the newspapers and plants," I say, my skin crawling and my stomach rumbling big-time.

"Oh, good. Eve's a real sweetheart. Comes from the gentile story, Adam and Eve and that snake in the garden. How much will you charge?"

I do some quick calculations, knowing she is in a bind and knowing that I might have to pay someone extra to entice them to feed Eve her rodents. After a while I name a figure.

There is a bloodcurdling shriek on the other end. "That's insane! That's highway robbery."

"The going price for tending a dog is thirty dollars a day," I say firmly. "I'm quoting you fifty. We're talking snake feeding here, watering plants, picking up papers and mail collection. It could be less if you purchase Eve's food in advance."

"How much less?"

I name a figure, shuddering all the while, picturing little white mice on their wheel in a cage. Imagine being raised exclusively for Eve's pleasure?

"I could arrange it if it would keep my cost down," Rona counters.

I am not sure I trust her. She sounds harried and high strung to me. Those mice could easily be running all over her home and my employee would be expected to capture them.

"The only thing you'll save is the cost of the food on your bill," I come back with.

She snorts, quibbles some more, and I give in some but not a lot. This is a two-week job. Why then do I feel I've been gotten over on?

I check the jobs on the schedule. They are pitifully few. Time to start drafting an idea for a New Year's promotion. Wife for Hire is known for prompt, personalized service. That is what we do best, and on that I will focus.

As I am jotting down thoughts, an idea comes to me. It is not exactly original, but if it works for the airlines, it can work for me.

I'll develop different price structures. I can offer discounts to those using the Web to order my services. I don't think that's going to be good enough, not if what

Rona says is true, and SNI is offering a two-for-the-price-of-one promotion. I need something really big. I can offer an introductory price to sample Wife for Hire. I can create payment plans for those customers who can't pay the full amount up-front. No, that is much too risky and I have no desire to float anyone or become a credit collector. I already have a few deadbeat customers.

Maybe a well-placed ad in Sunday's *Newsday* could help. I took out a loan and might as well use it. I need something bigger and better. Something to shake up the competitor. I need a big splash to make people open their wallets. Maybe I need to confer with a marketing consultant and see what they think.

Desperate times call for desperate measures. I need an innovative idea to pull my business out of this slump.

A shower will get my creative juices flowing, I decide. And in two hours I have a date with Delicious whose real name is Reed. He did call like he promised, and we are to meet at a nearby Starbucks. His efforts to come out to Long Island have gained him several points.

I spend a good twenty minutes under a hot shower and emerge with a clearer head. I am thinking that maybe the way to beef up business is to expand my services. I've already made a list of things most people hate to do. No one likes to clean toilets or organize closets. Filing paperwork is something we all dread. Most of us hate to stand in line, any line. But so far I've haven't come up with anything innovative. What I really need to do is hire that marketing guru.

I glance at the clock on my nightstand and realize the time has gotten away from me. I still don't know what I'm wearing. Choosing an outfit for a first date is always difficult, especially when you don't know the person's likes and dislikes. I decide to wear what I like. Take me or leave me.

I climb into black slacks which can be slimming, and slip a cream camisole over my head. I add a short tweed jacket to pull the whole thing together. Going for a youthful look, I sweep my hair with its burgundy highlights off my face and into a pretzel. I pluck at a few wisps around my hairline and I am almost ready. Silver hoop earrings, a hint of makeup and, presto, I am done.

I am jittery with anticipation. I've done this first meeting dozens of times, but this one feels different. Reed is different. There's been no cheesy lines or sexual come-ons. Reed hasn't asked prying questions nor has he gone the route of the Internet lingo. He's been a real gentleman and because of that he stands out.

A half hour later, I park the Land Rover in the Starbucks lot and quickly glance in the rearview mirror. I make sure there isn't a hint of this morning's breakfast stuck in my teeth nor is my lipstick bleeding. Reassured I am okay, I heave myself from the front seat.

What if there's no chemistry?

It is brutally cold, and steam curls from my open mouth and flaring nostrils. I wrap my scarf around my neck and hunker down into my coat's hood.

Better get this over with. I am hoping against all odds that Delicious is the one.

I enter the coffee shop and look around.

Is Delicious the man in the cabdriver cap, hunkered over a newspaper? Is he the guy in line who looks a little uncertain? Or is he the dude in the corner with an earpiece conducting an animated conversation with someone.

None of these men look even remotely like Reed's picture. But I am experienced enough to know that men in cyberland are caught up in the fantasy that they're younger than they look. The photos posted might even have come from a magazine.

I get online and order a latte but I am still looking around. I take the cup with me and sidle by a group of chatting people. I sidestep students with eyes glued to their laptops and find a table with a clear view of the entrance. I'm not concerned that it hasn't been bussed yet. At least I've found a place where we can sit.

I sweep a bunch of empty paper cups and lids into a nearby trashcan and grab a couple of napkins. I swipe at the table's surface before sitting down. Then, so as not to look anxious, I stick my nose into a newspaper that's left behind and pretend to be interested in an article.

The story ironically is about single women's choices in today's dating world. The paper lists the options, meaning: matchmaking, speed dating, singles parties and Internet dating. I am intrigued. There are many others like me out there hoping to make a connection.

Someone clears his throat behind me. I look over my shoulder. My heart jumps. Oh, boy, I like what I see.

"Roxi?" the man asks, carefully looking me over.

"Who's asking," I lob back. Reed is the spitting image of his picture.

He is hot and a lot taller than I expected. He has one of those lean, hard bodies that I like. His skin is weathered enough to indicate he has some life experience, and his hazel eyes are a nice contrast against his dark skin.

"Reed Samuels," he says, pulling out the chair across from me.

"Reed, at last," I manage.

He reaches over and takes my hand—the one not holding the latte and squeezes it gently.

A shiver skitters up my spine and down again. I feel like a teenager. Reed's complexion is the color of toasted almonds. His skin is tightly drawn across high cheekbones, and his light eyes hold me captive. He reminds me of the star athlete you meet years later at a class reunion who with age gets better. My insides are Jell-O.

"Roxi," Reed says, still holding on to my hand. "Interesting article?" He points to the newspaper.

"Actually, yes." I decide not to tell him that I am reading about people like us, reduced to meeting strangers via the Internet.

I fold up the paper and give him my full attention.

"How's your coffee holding up?" Reed asks.

"It's latte."

He stands. "I'll get you a refill and I'll get myself hot water." He reaches into the pocket of the ski jacket he's hung over the back of a chair and removes a packet holding a teabag. He sets it on the table.

Reed carries his own teabags. Hmm.

Boyfriend is definitely different. But there is a quiet elegance to him that I find most appealing and I can tell he is a man's man. I have come to the conclusion in a matter of these few minutes that I might easily fall in love with this man.

Reed's walk is loose-hipped and loose-jointed. He is completely unaffected by his looks. I think about Carlo briefly and then decide since I'm here with Reed Samuels who's looking for what I'm looking for—a long-term relationship—it's best to focus on him.

Reed returns to our table balancing two cups. He sets mine down in front of me, sits and plops a teabag into hot water.

"You're much cuter in person," he says, giving me a crooked smile that makes my heart jump.

"Thanks." He sounds sincere and not as if he's feeding me a line.

I still want to know why a man who looks like this one, with manners like this one, has resorted to posting an ad on the Internet. I want to know if he's wondering the same about me, and trying to figure out whether I have webbed feet or something. I take a big gulp and ask him.

"I posted an ad out of curiosity more than anything else," he says. "I wanted to see what would happen."

"And what has happened?"

"I met you." His voice is low and those hazel eyes are an alluring shade of steel.

I use my tongue to moisten my lips. I am flattered,

but it is much too soon to be this serious. I am also wondering if this is a line he feeds everyone he meets. I'm not into games and I sure hope that a man in his forties is over that.

We talk about what we enjoy doing when we aren't working. I am surprised at how similar our tastes are. I wonder if he's giving me the answers he thinks I want to hear. We are clicking away on every possible level. We both like good wine but don't want to pay a fortune for it. We enjoy hole-in-the–wall restaurants and ethnic foods. We drool over jazz from another era. And we share a fondness for old architecture.

I like cosmopolitans. He likes his martinis dry and with gin.

Reed laces his fingers through mine. He holds them in front of him, measuring the size of our hands.

"Have dinner with me," he says.

"When?"

I want to savor our meeting and think about him.

"This weekend."

"It's New Year's Eve," I remind him.

"Exactly. And I want to spend it with you."

Reed has just made a huge admission to me. He is free on the most important evening of the year; either that or some poor innocent woman is about to get dumped.

I don't want to think about being the cause of another woman's pain. But I like him and I don't have a thing planned. And it is New Year's Eve.

I can't be too eager. "Can I get back to you?" I ask. "I need to look at my calendar and move a few things around."

"Of course." He is still holding on to my hand. "Its gotten too crowded in here," he says. "Let's take a walk?"

I agree because for some inexplicable reason I am comfortable with him. I feel as if we have known each other forever.

He stands. I stand. We link hands and I walk out the door with him. Reed Samuels is what I have been looking for my entire life.

They say when you meet the right one you know.

Trust me, I know.

CHAPTER 14

I float home on a cloud and am still floating. My business worries are temporarily placed on the back burner. I have managed to get a date with a man I am attracted to and on New Year's Eve at that.

The red light on the answering machine is blinking when I enter my house. I am guessing it must be Margot. She'll want to know how my date with Reed went. We haven't had time to catch up. And I am afraid to call her in the event things did not go well with Earl.

When I depress the button, the male voice on the other end stops me in my tracks. "Happy holidays, Roxi. Hopefully its been a good one so far." My ex-husband, Kane. What does he want? It's been a while since I heard from him.

I take in a mouthful of air and compose myself. We've been divorced three years, but hearing his voice can still be an emotion-filled experience. We'd shared so much together.

"I'm trying to reach Lindsay," Kane says. "She's not answering her cell."

I know Lindsay told him she was moving to Paris. I'm wondering what this really is about. Kane had to know Lindsay's phone is disconnected. She'd seen him before she left and he'd given her money. I save the message to replay later and think about. I will call Kane back when I get around to it.

The next voice is Margot's. She's in one of her down moods, which means things did not go well. Earl has not been in touch with her since he came over Christmas evening. Now, that's a big surprise. But she is my friend, and despite her shortcomings she is usually there for me. I pick up the phone and hit speed dial.

"Where have you been?" Margot wails. "I really needed someone to talk to."

"I've been busy. Why are you so upset with Earl? You should be used to his disappearing acts."

"I thought it might be different this time."

She tells me how she and Earl ended up in bed together. That's another huge surprise.

I say. "Umm," and "Hmm," a lot.

"And now he's not returning my calls," she wails.

I make sympathetic noises. Now is definitely not the time to tell her how things went with Reed. I invite Margot for dinner and hang up. Next I pick up the phone and call a marketing company. The person I want to speak with is on vacation. An assistant tells me someone will get back to me after the holidays, which means after the first of the year.

I am curious if the competition is also experiencing a dip in business, but I am too chicken to use my cell phone to call. I find an old calling card and make sure my number is blocked. The phone gets picked up on the second ring.

"Service Not Incidental."

The voice is young and chirpy. It doesn't sound like Karen Miller's or Tamara Fisher's but it's been a while since I spoke to either of them. Just in case, I disguise my voice.

"I'm wondering if someone's available on New Year's Eve to take care of my dog, Muffy?" I ask.

"Hmm. That might be tough. Let's see how we are doing on appointments for New Year's Eve? Can you hold?"

While I am holding I am also holding my breath. What if she comes back and says she's full and unable to accommodate me?

I'm left on pins and needles for a full two minutes. I know, because I keep glancing at my watch.

"Where do you live?" she returns to ask.

Now I have to think quickly,

"The five-towns area. You must be busy, but I'd really appreciate it if you could fit me in."

"We are busy." I hear paper rustling and my anxiety goes up a notch. "Let me see where we can fit Muffy in."

Shit! If ten customers call with jobs on New Year's Eve I'd be kissing the ground not acting as if it's an imposition to accommodate them. Could they really be this busy? Based on their phone manners alone, their service is incidental.

"What about your two-for-the-price-of-one offer?" I ask. "I get another job free, right?"

"What about our two-for-one offer?" she counters.

"I need someone to take my car to the garage for an oil change."

Dead silence. In the background I hear muffled conversation.

"How far away is your mechanic?" she comes back on to ask.

I name a town not even five miles away.

"Sorry. Our two-for-the-price-of-one offer covers a one-mile radius." So that is the catch. "If you want us to feed your cat that's free, or do your grocery shopping, anything within one mile of the first job."

"What if you took my car to the local Jiffy whatchamacallit?" I ask.

"Hold for a sec."

Dead air again. Not, "Please hold for a moment,"

or "Would you mind holding for a moment?" Just a phone placed on hold, no music or anything.

After at least three minutes she comes back on the phone. "That's not possible. We can't risk the liability of driving your car."

Interesting. I pick up cars from train stations and airports all the time. I drive them from point A to B and I run them through car washes. So much for Service Not Incidental's two-for-one offer. Seems like a bit of a scam to me.

I tell the person I'll call back and I hang up. I begin preparing dinner. I put a bottle of pinot grigio into the refrigerator to chill. I will keep dinner simple. I'll make a chef salad and put tuna on the grill. I'm flipping the tuna when my phone rings, and I'm thinking of Reed. I reach for the landline without checking caller ID first.

Margot's voice comes at me. "I have to cancel," she says abruptly.

"Why, missie? I'm already cooking."

"Something's come up."

What's come up is probably Earl and his healthy libido.

"You were supposed to be here in an hour," I remind her.

"Yes, I know. Sorry, Roxi. I'll make it up to you another time."

I slam the phone down before I can say something truly horrible. I can refrigerate the tuna but this is an awful lot of salad for one person to eat. Maybe I can give my dinner to Jessica, the neighborhood terror's family. I find a Tupperware bowl and scoop most of the chef salad into it. I finish the tuna and wrap it in foil. Then I let myself out of the house, cross the street and ring the Applebaums' doorbell.

Jessica's mother opens the door. She is tall, elegant and fills out her jeans and a black turtleneck nicely. From her shocked expression, I can tell I am the last person she expects on her front step. So far we've had a nodding acquaintance. If Mr. Applebaum exists I've never seen him.

I explain why I'm here.

"That's so nice of you," she greets in an accented voice I can't place. "I'm Yvette, by the way." She stands aside and waves me in.

"I'm Roxi."

This is a first. I have never been in the Applebaums' house before. It is a Tudor like mine. Yvette works, or at least I assume she does, judging by when I see her leave home and return. And Jessica more often than not roams the neighborhood unsupervised, either that or she is beyond the babysitter's control.

The inside of Yvette's house is sparsely furnished. But what pieces there are, are expensive and tasteful.

"I've just opened a bottle of merlot, would you like a glass?" she asks.

"Love one."

We sit at her kitchen table, a huge oak piece with inlaid brass protected by a glass top.

"Where is Jessica?" I ask.

Yvette shrugs. "Impossible to tell. I can't keep up with that child and I can't keep her in the house. Since her father and I divorced she doesn't listen."

So that was the problem. No man in the house to keep an impressionable child in line and the mother is exhausted.

Yvette and I sip on our wine and make small talk. "You're a single woman, too, aren't you? What is it you do?"

I tell her. Yvette's eyes grow wide. "I am impressed. It has always been my dream to have my own business. I'd love to own a boutique that sells fashionable clothes."

"What do you do?" I ask her.

She sighs. "I waitress now, helps with the bills. In my country I majored in accounting but my degree is useless in the United States. Waitressing is the only thing I could find when I was forced to get out there again. I'm a cocktail waitress at this restaurant in Freeport. Tips are good but customers suck."

I sympathize with her. Being on your feet for hours

has to be brutal, plus getting hit on by paunchy, balding players, isn't anyone's idea of fun.

"Where's the accent from?" I ask, although I now have a pretty good idea.

"I'm French but I've lived in the States a really long time. I think no one notices anymore."

We talk some more. I tell her that Lindsay is in Paris trying to become proficient in French and trying her hand at a modeling career. Yvette tells me how much life has changed since her divorce. I listen but she's singing to the choir. My life's changed, too, and all for the better. I'm in control now, responsible and accountable for my own actions. My daughter, Lindsay's, grown and capable of making her own decisions. She'll have to accept the consequences of any rash behavior.

I suddenly get an idea. Maybe I should hire Yvette to work for me. I can tell she hates her job, and I need reliable, dependable people. Plus, she's right next door. Customers, especially men, are going to love that accent. If I have a righthand person it will free me up to work with the marketing company. I need to put Wife for Hire back on the map.

Maybe Yvette and I can help each other out.

"How would you feel about working for me?" I ask.

"In what capacity?" she asks, her gold-flecked eyes wide.

I describe what I want her to do. She's to handle the phone calls, deal with difficult people, set up schedules and straighten out the books.

"I accept," she says before I can even finish.

"But I haven't even told you how much I'd pay you."

"Tell me over dinner. You will stay, won't you? We'll have your chef salad and that delicious-looking tuna."

I am about to protest, but Yvette holds up her hand silencing me. The other picks up the receiver of the wall phone.

"Let me call around and see if I can find Jessica. That child gives me premature gray hairs."

Yvette shakes a full mane of chestnut hair that has escaped its rubber band at me. I don't see one silver strand.

She gets a lead on Jessica and hangs up. "Now, what is it you were saying about salary?"

I have now hired another employee. And something tells me she is going to be good.

New Year's Eve arrives sooner than I've anticipated. Meanwhile I've been busy planning parties and making sure caterers deliver what they are supposed to. In between, I've spoken to Reed twice. I am liking him more and more. He isn't as charismatic as Carlo, but he is kind, smart and has good manners. He tells me he is an architect and that he's been divorced twice. The red flag should be fluttering but it isn't. Things happen.

So here I am two hours before our date, agonizing over what I'm going to wear. Margot is sitting on the edge of my bed, chastising me.

"How come you didn't try several outfits on days ago?" she chides. "Where is he taking you, anyway?"

I don't have a clue. I've taken a big gamble and given him my home address; something I never do. But I've met Reed and I've had an attorney friend run a background check on him. He's checked out, so I feel pretty confident that he isn't an ax murderer. The only thing we haven't been able to verify is if he's officially divorced. I'm figuring he has to at least be separated, because no woman in her right mind is going to let her man out of sight on New Year's Eve.

Margot has agreed to stick around until Reed picks me up. She claims to have plans for later; a house party or something; probably with Earl, if he doesn't stand her up. Something tells me he and his other woman are on the outs.

I toss a handful of clothing on the bed beside Margot.

"Come on, help me pick. I need to look elegant but not overdressed."

"Why not overdressed? It's New Year's Eve, probably the one time you can afford to break out the satin, sequins and furs. You don't really know this guy. You should be ready for anything."

It takes us another fifteen minutes to make a selection. I settle on a black-off-the shoulder dress and dress it up with a glittery shrug. I wear high-heeled strappy sandals with rhinestone buckles. It's cold outside and my feet are probably going to feel like blocks of ice.

Bacci is howling loudly as if sensing something is up. Perhaps she knows I am about to step out on Carlo.

"What's up with that cat?" Margot asks, making a face. She has never been much of an animal lover.

I finish my makeup, sweep my hair off my face and put on my good jewelry.

As Margot is helping with the clasp on my necklace the doorbell rings.

I take a deep breath and send Margot off to get it.

I can't wait to see Reed again.

CHAPTER 15

"Well, what do you think so far?" Reed asks as we are standing in the lobby of the theater during intermission, clutching two champagne flutes and sipping slowly.

Earlier we've had dinner and now we are at the show.

"The lead is giving an electrifying performance. He's a Thespian trained in the classics, did you know?"

"No, I didn't know."

The lobby of the Algonquin Theater is packed, and despite my efforts to dress up, I am feeling underdressed. There are people in black tie and ankle-length gowns. One dowager is actually wearing a tiara and there are men in tuxedos and satin bow ties. There is one man strutting around in a top hat, carrying a silver cane.

Reed places an arm around me and brings me closer. He looks very handsome in his black double-breasted jacket and gray flannel slacks. His collar is open and I can smell a very subtle cologne that makes me think of Christmas. We are getting along so well it's actually scary. Reed anticipates my every move and seems to know what to do and say. There is a boyish charm to him that is very appealing. He makes no bones of letting me know he is interested in me. I am eating up all the attention. It feels good to be someone's fantasy.

"We have that house party afterward," he reminds me, "I hope you'll still be up for it. I'm looking forward to introducing you to my friends."

I smile at him. I am excited and pleased that I mean enough to him that he is letting me into his life. Earlier he mentioned the host lives on Park Avenue, in a building well known for its celebrity tenants. I am hoping to rub elbows with some prominent pop stars, a *New York Times* bestselling author and maybe a model or two.

The lights in the lobby dim, signaling time to take our box seats again. Reed has gone all out this evening to show me a good time. It must be costing him a fortune. I watch the rest of the show with his arm around me. I feel as if we've known each other a lifetime. When I sniff through the sad parts of the show, he kisses my cheek.

"You know what I like about you?" he whispers. I shake my head. "You're smart, independent but still vulnerable."

Those kind words make me sniff even more. I've never had a man be so open and honest with me.

The play finally ends and the lights go up. The

actors get a standing ovation. We leave and at my insistence—Reed would have come back to get me— we walk two freezing blocks to the garage where he has parked his Saab.

Twenty minutes later I am dropped off in front of a swanky apartment building and turned over to a door-man. I wait in the lobby for Reed who's gone to park the car.

I look around the white on white lobby with the im-pressive columns and low brocaded divans, and I think money, lots of it. I admire signed artwork, wondering how the management company dared leave originals here. They must be well insured I decide.

Reed comes sailing through the smoked-glass re-volving doors with confidence. His hazel eyes roam the area looking for me. My breath gets caught in my throat. I think this man with the threads of silver run-ning through his hair is breathtakingly beautiful, and with a gentleness to him that can't be beat. He will calm me down when I get hyper.

When Reed spots me his eyes light up. He throws an arm around my shoulders and my stomach actually does flip-flops. This hasn't happened since high school. And I'd begun to think it isn't possible.

"Let's go get a drink," he says, leading me toward the elevator.

Another couple comes racing across the lobby shouting in unison, "Hold the elevator."

They are wearing silly hats and sequined glasses, the kind that spell out the new year. They carry noisemakers and a wrapped gift for the hostess. They get on the elevator and I can tell they have already been partying.

Reed dutifully stabs the button when they are safely in.

"Penthouse, please," the male half says to Reed, one finger in the air.

"Already done."

They eye us speculatively. The female says, "Are you going to the same party we are?"

"Could be," Reed answers cryptically.

We smile at each other and then the lift stops. Reed takes my hand and we exit, treading our way across plush carpeting and down a long hall. I still have no idea whose party this is, but what I do know is that anyone who can afford to live here has money. Raised voices greet us before we even approach the door. If the other penthouses haven't been invited there will be complaints.

Before we can ring the bell, the door pushes open. It is the first time I have seen a butler up close and personal. The round-faced solemn-looking man in tails intimidates me.

Reed sails us by him, "Hey, what's up, Hadley? Isn't my date beautiful?" He knows what to say. He makes me feel like a million bucks.

I float along with renewed confidence and tread my way through the wall of people. The place is packed and the smell of champagne is in the air. Tuxedoed waiters and waitresses squeeze themselves between guests, platters held high in the air. We lose our couple in the crush.

"We'll grab a drink and go find our host and hostess," Reed says close to my ear. He smoothly navigates me around groups of chattering people. Finding the host is easier said than done.

The bars have people three lines deep, making it impossible to get drinks anytime soon. We settle for the champagne the waitstaff is serving. Reed lifts two flutes off a tray and passes one over.

"Whose party are we attending?" I ask while sipping.

He names a singing duo famous in the eighties that currently own a restaurant.

"Wow!" I say. "I had no idea you moved in such circles."

"I've known them awhile," he says. "I designed their first house."

My mouth opens and closes. And just in time, too, because we finally spot our host outside on the rooftop garden surrounded by people. He is tall and lean and his hair now is shorter. I remember him from concerts when he had flowing locks and women tried to lure him away from his wife by tossing their underwear onstage. There is no sign of his petite, attractive wife amongst the group chatting. We make our way over and stand on the periphery of his admirers, hoping to catch his eye.

Finally he sees us.

"Reed, glad you made it, man." He nods at me. "Your taste is definitely improving."

I am introduced and Nick and Reed talk some more. Then Nick moves on to find his wife. This leaves us to weave our way through an animated crowd in search of food.

The buffets are filled to capacity. And although I am still full from dinner I must sample the Alaskan king crab and at least one of the miniquiches. As time passes people become increasingly merrier. Soon champagne and noisemakers are passed out, and we bring in the new year singing "Auld Lang Syne" and kissing each other. Reed kisses me on the mouth, a real kiss, our tongues dip and circle. When he finally lets up I feel as if I have grown wings and can fly. It must be the champagne talking.

A half an hour later, the crowd is thinning out and

Reed and I thank our hosts. After promising to come back for dinner we climb aboard a crowded elevator. Reed again leaves me in the lobby and goes to get the car.

While he's gone, a drunken male wobbles over. I'd seen him making his way around the party chatting up a number of women.

"Want to go home with me?" he asks.

"Sorry, not tonight. I'm already taken."

"You're no fun," he slurs.

I look around frantically hoping that the man who can barely stand has friends, a spouse, someone. He is in no condition to drive.

"Know who I am?" he continues.

He does look vaguely familiar, but frankly, I don't care. His breath is enough to ignite a fire.

Reed pulls up out front, thank God. I make a run for it, stopping to plead with the doorman, "Please put that man in a cab. He shouldn't be driving."

Reed pats my knee when I slide into the passenger seat. He wiggles his eyebrows. "So, do you want to come see my etchings?"

He is cute. My insides go all fluttery, but it's too soon to sleep with him. I know only what he's told me, and personal details have been far and few. I have met his friends and that counts for something. But can I really believe that he is who he says he is? My Internet experiences make me skeptical. Reality is often far different from what you see on the surface.

I know I like Reed, and although he is not Carlo, he makes my engines rev. But things are happening too fast. I need to slow them down. I have my heart to consider. What if this is his modus operandi: get a woman interested then move on?

Reed pinches the flesh above my kneecap. "Am I moving too fast?" he asks, putting what I'm thinking into words.

He doesn't sound as confident now.

"I don't want to be a quick hit," I say. "I'm not interested in a quick hop in the sack."

"I'm not talking sex. I was hoping you'd come home with me and we'd drink more champagne and watch the sun come up together."

Now, that sounds very tempting to me. I've already brought in a new year with this man. Still, my caution buttons are on high. Reed and me alone in his apartment? He could be a serial killer, for all I know. And what if I can't stop myself from jumping his bones?

"I need to call my girlfriend and tell her where I'll be," I say, just in case. "What's your address?"

Reed gives it to me and hands me his cell phone.

How sweet is that?

* * *

His apartment overlooks the East River. The furniture, what little there is, has nice lines and is expensive. Reed has the requisite sectional couch and coffee table in his living room. He has one of those pricey plasma televisions mounted on the far wall. His kitchen is galley-style and the appliances actually look used. There are cookbooks lined up on the counter and gadgets hanging from the ceiling that I have no idea how to use. I may have found myself a gourmet chef. Another plus in his favor.

He pours us glasses of champagne and then gives me the tour: bathroom, bedroom, study, all equally austere. I notice several bows and arrows in one room and wonder about them. Before I can ask, I hear a whining, scratching noise and say, "Are you holding someone hostage?"

Reed smiles and takes my hand. "Come meet Guinness."

I look at him curiously.

"He's my killer dog."

He opens the door to the laundry room and the hugest beast I've seen in a long time comes bounding out, tongue hanging from his mouth. The dog begins slurping on him.

"Down, Guinness," Reed says.

The dog's attention turns to me, and now I am the beneficiary of several wet kisses.

Feeling an immediate bond, I hug Guinness around the neck. His long pink tongue darts out, covering me in slobber.

"Guinness adores you," Reed says, stating the obvious. "He is a very good judge of character."

I accept a few more wet kisses, and then the dog settles down. He spreads out on the floor of Reed's den and looks at me adoringly.

"Stay, boy," Reed says, linking an arm around my waist. "Come. I want you to hear something." I follow him through the apartment wondering what it is that I am to listen to. Reed flips on the stereo to a smooth jazz station. He pats the sofa motioning for me to sit. "Be right back."

I sip my champagne and listen to Earl Kluge play a mean guitar. Reed comes back with guitar case in hand. He lowers the music, takes out the instrument and begins strumming before breaking out in full song. I think I have died and gone to heaven. In the back of my mind I am thinking this man is too perfect. There must be something wrong with him.

I'll relax and live in the moment. I have never had any man serenade me before, and certainly not one that looks like Reed Samuels. He puts his guitar away and comes to sit beside me. Reed gathers me in his arms and kisses the top of my head.

"How are you holding up?"

"I'm a little tired."

"So am I," he says, yawning loudly.

Here it comes. I should have expected it, but I'd come up to his apartment voluntarily and should be prepared.

"Perhaps we should lie down for a moment and catch a few winks."

I remain silent but my expression says it all.

"I won't touch you unless you want me to."

The funny thing is that now I do want him to. Still, in the back of my mind I'm thinking, he needs to work a little bit if he wants me. I remember something my mother once told me, no woman should give it up that easily.

Reed stands up and reaches out a hand. I take it. I follow him up the hallway and into a room that is more vanilla than the living room. All of the furniture is blond. The bed matches the dresser, which matches the nightstand. The walls are bare and there are few personal effects in sight. What's up with that I wonder?

Fully clothed, we slide under the covers. Reed wraps me in his arms. He even smells like vanilla. When he kisses me I taste his champagne. I snuggle up next to him and rest my head on his chest. He strokes my hair.

When I open my eyes the room is coated in sunshine. So much for staying awake to watch the sun rise, but we have gotten through this and managed not to have sex. Reed kisses the top of my head then sticks his legs out from under the comforter and plants them firmly on the floor.

"I'm starving," he says. "We should think about breakfast." He walks into the bathroom and closes the door.

My mouth is feeling as if a sewer erupted in it. I dare not open it. I need a shower, and since I didn't plan this to be an overnight adventure, I wonder how to handle a change of clothes.

Fifteen minutes later Reed is back bearing towels and a new toothbrush. He opens closet doors and hands me a sweatsuit.

"Not sure I can manage underwear," he says, smiling, "unless you would like to wear mine." He shakes a package of briefs at me.

Hand over my mouth, I mutter my thank-you and grab the stuff. I head for the bathroom and the shower. I brush my teeth and recycle my underwear. It is much too intimate a gesture to think about wearing his, new or otherwise. I bunch up the arms and legs of the sweatsuit after I put it on.

My hair is all frizzy from the steam of the shower. I pinch my cheeks and put on lip gloss. Then I gaze in the mirror, thinking how odd I look in Reed's oversize sweats with my strappy sandals from the night before. Reed's feet have to be at least a size twelve—no hope of borrowing his sneakers.

He is in the kitchen making omelets that smell heavenly. There is toast in the toaster and coffee dripping from the pot. A huge bowl of fruit is already on the table. Reed stops flipping the omelet to kiss my cheek. He hands me a bottle of springwater.

"I was thinking of taking you to brunch, but thought it might be cozier to stay in," he says. "You look wonderful in that sweatsuit."

The man is blind. Then again if he thinks I look good in oversize clothes and no makeup he just might be a keeper.

He finishes what he's doing, turns off the stove and takes me with him to the window. We stand staring out on the East River and the few boats making their way slowly up and down. Come spring and summer the river will be crowded with party boats.

"I loved having you next to me," Reed whispers in my ear.

"Me, too. It felt natural, comfortable."

He kisses me. This time a real kiss. Long, deep and meaningful. At least, I think it is meaningful. My head spins as I kiss him back.

My cell phone rings and I go instantly on the alert. I press my palms against his chest forcing us apart. I am thinking maybe it's Lindsay.

The phone is in my purse. I hurry to find it. The ringing stops before I get to it. I hit the missed call button and Margot's name pops up. I hear the ping notifying me that a message has been left. What now? It is early for her to be up.

Reed meanwhile is getting breakfast on the table.

I retrieve the message. Margot's high-pitched keening greets me. My euphoric moment is over.

"Roxi, I need you," she wails. "Where exactly are you again?"

And with that, stone-cold reality returns.

I am hesitant to tell Margot that I am still at Reed's.

"What's wrong?" I ask, knowing that once that door is open this conversation could go on for hours. And I don't have hours. My eggs are waiting. I smell buttery croissants and dark roasted coffee. The combined aromas make my stomach grumble.

"I woke up this morning and Earl was gone," Margot says between sniffs.

"I'd think he'd have to get home." I bit back the words on the tip of my tongue. What does she expect of a man who's involved with another woman?

"There was no note. Nothing. He just left."

"Okay, take a deep breath. Breathe."

"Easy for you to say. Where are you, anyway? I drove to your house but you weren't home. I need you."

Although he doesn't interrupt, I know Reed is waiting. I also know he is tuned in to the conversation.

"I'll stop by your house later. We'll have a mimosa and toast to a better year."

I hang up quickly and take the chair Reed holds out. He pours us both coffee and dishes an omelet onto my plate. He even butters my toast. Then he places a pitcher of orange juice in the center of the table and takes his seat. Guinness is sprawled on his back under the table. He doesn't whine and he doesn't beg.

Although I don't owe Reed an explanation I begin to explain.

"She sounds lonely," Reed said with amazing insight.

"That she is. Margot measures her worth in terms of a man. Unfortunately she's not over Earl and probably never will be. And he encourages the codependency."

"Sounds like a pretty dysfunctional pair."

"They are."

Reed begins to talk about himself. I hear about his parents passing at an early age and how he basically raised himself. I hear about his two failed marriages, both of which were brief. My antenna goes up again. I wonder why he can't sustain a relationship. Someone who looks like him, has a decent job and a caring personality, is every woman's dream.

Breakfast is over with. We have eaten everything including the fruit. I don't want to overstay my welcome. I tell Reed I'll take the Long Island Railroad home but he won't hear of it.

"I'll drive you back, but I wish you would stay longer," he says. "If we're going to be spending time together. I might as well see how you live."

I keep my expression neutral but he's blown me away. It sounds to me as if he intends for this to be an ongoing thing. That is A-okay with me. As I said before, I like this man.

There is a dusting of snow on the highway when he drives me back to Long Island. Reed drives with one hand, the other is on my leg. I feel comfortable with him. He's what I've been waiting for my entire life: kind, attentive and respectful of me.

We pull up in front of my Tudor and he gets out and

comes around to the passenger door and gives me his hand. I am hoping that my house is in good shape and that Bacci hasn't urinated on the floor or shredded the upholstery. Alexandra is supposed to come and get him tomorrow. I'd hoped it would be Carlo but I've gotten over that. Funny how little thought I've given to a man that I'd been obsessing over for years.

"I've always liked this town," Reed says as he walks me to my door.

"You know Malverne?" I give him my are-you-shitting-me-or-what? look and wait for more.

He places a hand on my arm. "I've had an occasion or two to come out here," he says, straight-faced.

Until then, I haven't thought of the possibility he might be seeing someone. When you meet a man on the Internet that is just the way that it goes.

We stand on the landing. I have my keys out.

"Would you like to come in?" I ask.

"Absolutely."

With that Reed enters my house. Margot and her emergency are placed on the back burner.

I need to cultivate this relationship, develop it into more.

CHAPTER 16

The holidays are finally over but business sucks big-time. I am willing to pretty much do anything to keep afloat—even discount my services. I've met with the marketing consultant and together we've come up with a concept called January Madness. The idea being you pay a flat, nominal fee for any service, and the remainder is due thirty days later. If you don't pay in full after the grace period there is a premium. This involves some level of trust, and I hope I will not live to regret this crazy marketing decision. The good thing is I get the credit card up-front and I have the customer's signature that he will be charged.

My across-the-street neighbor, Yvette Applebaum is aboard and doing quite well. I am used to being a one-man band, but Yvette is good at taking pressure off. I trust her to answer phones, create schedules and take care of jobs that require a certain level of diplomacy. As predicted, the delightful French accent is going over big.

I have heard from Reed every day and we are getting

closer. I like the attention and support. Now I hardly ever think about Carlo, who incidentally sent me a wonderful note to thank me for caring for Bacci. He really is a sweet man and considerate.

I am in the middle of ordering dessert for a dinner party when my cell phone rings. I allow it to go to voice mail until I negotiate the price and complete the transaction. My client will be pleased. Fresh strawberries are exactly what she wanted, and those are hard to come by in winter without paying a small fortune for them.

I wait until I'm in the Land Rover to check my message. It is Reed. My heart does a triple beat when I hear his voice.

"Hello, doll. I've just scored tickets for the symphony tonight. Tell me you are free."

I call him back. I am free and very much looking forward to seeing him. We decide I will take the train in and meet him at his apartment. We will have drinks and dinner before the symphony.

After I get off, I call Margot and find her in a surprisingly upbeat mood.

"Have you heard from Earl?" I ask cautiously because usually Margot's good moods are associated with Earl contacting her.

"No, but I've heard from Theo."

"Who?"

"Dr. Theodore Fitzpatrick. The guy I met at the lock-and-key party, remember him?"

"Oh, yeah, him. What's with him?"

Theo is the homie with the heavy urban accent that I suspect Margot went home with. Hopefully he is single. But at this point anyone is better than Earl, who can't seem to leave Margot alone or make up his mind.

Margot is rambling on telling me that Theo has asked her out to dinner. It's taken him several weeks to ask her out. What's with that? Sounds to me as if he's just been dumped or why is he suddenly available?

I force enthusiasm into my voice. "That's nice. So where are you two going?"

Margot names a well-known restaurant which is a bit on the pricey side. It sounds as if the doc is willing to invest a dollar or two. I become hopeful again. Margot needs a break.

I tell Margot I have to go. I need to figure out what to wear to the symphony. I've not been invited to attend this type of event before. The closest I've come is a front-row seat on my couch, staring at the television.

When I enter my house, my cell phone rings. I heave out a breath, thinking, Margot again.

"Hello, princess." I don't quite get the voice.

"Who's this?"

"How was your holiday?"

"Fine, and yours?"

"It's Max. How soon we forget."

He is acting as if nothing has happened, as if he hasn't just disappeared on me. This is the man who'd supposedly come to New York to spend the holiday with me. I wait for an explanation, an excuse. Something.

"I'm flying out to catch the ship in a couple of days and thought we might get together."

The unmitigated gall of him.

"Sorry, Max. I can't." I say. There is no explanation for his callous, self-focused behavior, and I don't feel I owe him a thing. What's more, I don't want to see him.

"Oh, come on," Max wheedles. "I really would like to see my favorite girl."

"I'm busy."

"You've never been too busy for me before," Max says.

I decide this is going around in circles. We are clearly going nowhere, just like our relationship is not going anywhere. Max has served a purpose. He has helped me transition from divorcée to more-confident single woman. It is time to cut the strings, and it is time for me to be straight so there's no misunderstanding.

"Max," I say. "Despite you giving me a lot of lip service about being here for me, I haven't heard from you in weeks."

Long sigh on the other end. "So that's the problem."

"A big one for me. I need friends I can rely on."

"Whoa!" he says. "And you can't rely on me?"

"I can't depend or rely on you, and that's a big problem for me."

I can hear the wheels turning, and I am not feeling very patient.

"I have to go, Max," I say. "I have things to take care of."

I hang up.

I am a little sad because having Max as a friend was nice while it lasted. Now I am at a different place altogether. When you are looking for a potential long-term mate you need someone as solid as a rock, not someone floating in and out of your life when it pleases him.

I go into my closet looking for something to wear tonight. Twenty minutes and several discarded outfits later I decide on simple but classic. I choose a full, ankle-length black skirt and an ivory silk top. I accessorize with pearls and add a black satin belt at the waist, the type that has a bow where a buckle should be.

I decide to take a bath and spend a half hour luxuriating in bubbles. I get out before I turn into a prune and begin the business of dressing. Then I sweep my hair off my face, twist it into another of those pretzels and add a sparkly comb. My makeup is simple, just a touch of foundation, some blush and mascara. I step into black pumps, grab a red pashmina and I am ready to go.

The train is on time. I take a cab from Penn Station to Reed's apartment. He has left a message with his doorman to expect me. His door is ajar when I get off the elevator.

"Anyone home," I call, not wanting to just walk in.

Guinness comes bounding out of the bedroom. He licks my hand, but well-trained dog that he is, does not jump. Reed follows, looking devastatingly handsome in a dark suit, his shirt open at the collar, his hair still wet and in tight little salt-and-pepper ringlets.

"Just look at you," he says. "Beautiful as always." He kisses me on the mouth and when we come up for air he says, "Make yourself comfortable. I'll be out in a minute." He waves me toward the sofa.

Guinness follows me and sits at my feet. I stare out at the East River and the twinkling lights of the far shore. A jazz guitarist plays mood music in the background. So far everything is perfect.

Reed's house phone rings and rings. He doesn't pick it up. I make out a female voice but can't hear the message. I'm not particularly bent out of shape because he is a good-looking man with a great job, and it's natural that there would be women. And we haven't had the talk about exclusivity.

When Reed returns, his hair is dry. "We could stay in and have drinks here if you'd like," he offers.

I shake my head. I am intensely attracted to this man and if we don't go out we'll never make it to the symphony.

Outside, Reed's doorman flags us down a taxi. We decide it's quicker and more efficient. This way we don't have to deal with traffic and parking. Reed folds a bill into the doorman's palm before we get in.

We are dropped off about two blocks away from Carnegie Hall. Reed has reservations at a new restaurant that has received wonderful reviews. It is one of those chi-chi places with warm dark wood, plush carpeting and cavernous banquettes. It smells like pine and cranberries.

After telling the maître d' who we are, Reed takes my elbow. We follow a hostess, sidestepping an affluent after-work crowd, knocking back drinks. Reed exchanges nods with several of the men. Finally we are taken to a table in the back.

As we wait for the waitress to come over, Reed asks, "So what is it you like to do when you're not running a business?"

"I play tennis, work out at the gym, travel when there's disposable income, and now I'm thinking of taking a watercolor class. What about you?"

"I play squash and racquetball. I fence and horse-back ride every chance I get. I'm also an archer."

All gentlemen's games. That explains the collection of bows and arrows I've seen at Reed's home.

"How did you get into archery?" I ask.

"My father was an archer. He used to take me to the range with him. He wasn't a very demonstrative man so that was the way we bonded."

Reed's cell phone rings. He glances at the number and snaps the phone off.

"You could have answered," I said. "I wouldn't have been insulted."

"Not important."

The waitress comes and takes our drink order. We talk about one thing or another. Reed tells me that he's thought about me a lot and how much he enjoys my company.

We have dinner. We go to the symphony. Reed keeps his arm around me the whole time. Afterward he runs into some people he knows and introduces me. This is another good sign. I interpret it as me being around for a while. He asks me to go home with him. I say yes. I am fully aware of what I am doing. I am violating my own three-date rule. Three dates before I consider going to bed with a man.

We take another taxi back to the Eastside. Guinness greets us at the door. He needs to be walked. Reed gets the dog's leash and I accompany him back downstairs. Guinness does his business and we climb back on the elevator again.

"Can you stay the night?" Reed asks when Guinness is curled into a ball back in his laundry room.

I hesitate before answering. I expected him to ask and now that he has, I'm nervous. Not nervous of Reed but scared of my feelings, because they are that intense, and it is all happening too fast.

"You've spent the night before so you've got to know I won't force myself on you," he says as his home phone rings. He trots off to answer.

Reed's in the kitchen. I hear him pick up the phone and then slam it down again. I didn't know he has a temper.

"Was that a crank call?" I ask when he comes back.

"Something like that." The brackets around his mouth tighten.

The phone rings again. He snorts loudly, mutters something and goes into the kitchen. The same thing happens. Reed returns with two glasses of wine and hands one to me.

"Maybe you should call the police," I say, when he says nothing by way of explanation.

"No police. Not necessary."

It pops into my head that maybe this is someone he's avoiding. Not my problem.

He pulls me to my feet and takes me with him to the floor-to-ceiling windows. We look out on the night and the occasional boat as it journeys up the river. Using one hand to hold his wineglass, he embraces me with the other.

"So you'll stay," he says close to my ear. "I'm liking you more and more, Roxi, and I'm in this for the long haul." He begins nibbling on my earlobe.

I can feel the heat coming off his skin and I can smell the clean fresh smell of his skin. We aren't kids. I know when it's right, and this feels right to me. And so I ignore the little voice in my head that says there is something strange about these phone calls.

Reed's fingers are massaging the side of my arm. His heated breath is on my neck. His lips tug at my skin. He sets both of our wineglasses down on a nearby table and pulls me into his arms.

"I want to love you all over," he says, his voice husky and deeper than the Reed I know.

It is my hand that reaches for his shirt buttons. They are my fingers that trace a pattern across his undershirt and over his hardened nipples. It is me who presses into him.

He is cupping my buttocks and rubbing against me, showing me just how much I am turning him on. I feel my nipples pebble and I feel my body throb. When Reed plucks at my blouse, pulling it from my skirt, I don't stop him. I feel the heat of his palms against my bare midriff, and the tips of his fingers scorch as they dive under the lace of my bra and graze my breasts.

"We should take this into the bedroom," Reed says, breathlessly.

I manage a nod and a noise that can be interpreted as "Yes."

I gather my gaping blouse and, breathing heavily, follow him up the hallway.

Guinness lets out a "woof" as we pass the laundry room and then he settles down.

In Reed's room the comforters are already folded at the bottom of his bed. It is as if he expected this. The lamps on the nightstands are dimmed and the room is coated in a yellow hue. With Reed's help, I climb out of my clothes. When he is nude he places an arm around my waist and lifts me onto the bed. We wrap ourselves around each other, forehead to forehead.

Not a word is said, but the intimacy of our connection cannot be disputed. Reed's erection presses into my stomach. His breath comes in little pants. His hands are roaming my body exploring the nooks and crannies. I return the favor, exploring his hardening flesh. Reed rolls me onto my back and parts my legs. He is on his knees and his head is between my thighs.

I am afire, my body ignited by a need as ancient as time. As his tongue dips and dances, he takes me to additional heights. I shift position, pleasuring him just as he is pleasuring me. Reed sighs. His hips buck and do a full rotation as I take him firmly in my mouth. I am excited because he is excited.

He flips me on my side and places his member between my thighs. We move back and forth until I am whimpering. Reed's hands cup my breasts and trail my nipples. His slightly chapped lips nip my skin. Reed's hands are everywhere, his fingers probing my orifices. I buck against him telling him I am ready.

He slips on a condom and seconds later is inside of me. I hold on to him fast with quivering muscles. Reed shudders then plunges even deeper into me. An arm circles my waist holding me firm. We are butt to belly when Reed ramps up the motion. I am tingling everywhere and each nerve is alive.

Now he is grunting and I am grunting right along

with him. Even my lips are gyrating. I am past the point of no return. I feel the warmth, the heaviness in my center, and know I am about to explode.

"Come with me," Reed says as his body begins to spasm. I am more than ready. I let go.

I can no longer hear him. I am overflowing with sensations and all I can do is feel. And then I hear me scream.

Reed holds me tight and we fall into a place of sweet delight. A place where only sensations matter.

We are in sync, connected on yet another level.

CHAPTER 17

"Anything I can do to help?" Yvette asks when she finds me hunched over the computer the next day.

"Find me a whole new set of customers that want to spend money," I say laughingly.

"Everything in its time. They will come."

She gives me a wide smile and squeezes my shoulder. My face must say it all. I am going to have a hard time making payroll this month, and none of my self-talk is making me feel any better. I am also thinking about Reed. Last night's lovemaking was just surreal.

This could be a temporary lull in business, which is fairly typical in the weeks following the holiday, but I am not so sure. A few loyal customers have disappeared, and I have a fairly good idea where they might have danced off to. Service Not Incidental.

I need to do something and quickly. I need results from that January Madness mailing. It is going to take a full week before I know what the impact is, and meanwhile I am going to have to juggle bills and that's something I hate.

My doorbell rings, an unwelcome distraction right now. I sigh loudly and go off to answer.

"Who is it?"

"Florist."

Must be the wrong house. I can't think of a reason for anyone to send me flowers. I ask the man for his ID, check it out and carefully open the door. A huge bouquet is thrust at me. It is one of those exotic arrangements with orchids, birds of paradise, ginger lilies and trailing ferns. It has to have cost a small fortune.

The deliveryman lingers waiting for his tip. I find my purse and fumble through it. I give him several dollars before removing the card. A huge smile breaks out on my face as I realize the sender is Reed.

Yvette comes up behind me as I am hugging the bouquet to my chest.

"How beautiful. You have an admirer," she says.

"I would like to think so."

I have not discussed my business with her but the expression on my face must be dreamy. I am still bowled over by the intensity of last night's lovemaking. And now Reed has gone out of his way to let me know I am more than just a fling. I will think about what this all means later. Right now I have more pressing issues. I have a business that may be in serious trouble.

I put the flowers in their accompanying urn on the mantel where I can see them. Then I search my database. I need to try to drum up repeat business. Maybe I can reach out to customers that have been inactive for a year or more. I will e-mail them and offer discounted services if they sign on again.

While Yvette returns to her scheduling, I do a quick check of unread mail. Why is Vance e-mailing me? I click onto his mail and I bite my lip to calm down. He is resigning and doesn't say why. I feel a sense of betrayal. What about his talk of loyalty and the fact his mother will have his behind. Really, this couldn't come at a worse time. Vance performs a lot of the tedious duties no one else wants to do. He has an infinite amount of patience and doesn't mind waiting in long lines.

I grab the phone and call him but he doesn't pick up. Coward! I take a deep breath and decide to look at the positive. Having him quit means one person off the payroll, and that should help ease the financial burden a bit. Margot can be counted on in a pinch providing she's available. And she doesn't expect to be paid.

I see an e-mail address I do not recognize. There is nothing particularly strange about this, but something about the screen name sets off alarm bells in my head.

I don't know a BetteBeautiful@yahoo.com. But I do have good virus protection so I click on the message and quickly scan it. It is most likely just spam.

It is a very convoluted story about a woman whose ex-husband takes up with someone else. The woman is forced out of her house but before she leaves she has a last supper and tucks her shrimp shells in the curtain rods. What the hell is this all about? My gut tells me to save this message.

I read my other mail but I am still distracted by the odd message which keeps replaying itself in my head. There is also an e-mail from Max. I read it quickly. He is trying for a comeback and is both contrite and apologetic. He still offers no explanation for his disappearance.

Max tells me how much he cares about me and how much our friendship means to him. It is too little and too late. He has served a purpose. He has gotten me through a difficult period in my life and I will forever be grateful to him. I need someone more reliable and dependable. I need someone like Reed.

Yvette enters from the outer room. She holds the office phone in one hand. I didn't even hear it ring.

"There's a gentleman asking for you," she says. "Wants to speak only to you."

I frown. "He wouldn't give you his name?"

"Carlo, I think. I didn't catch his last name."

My heart jumps. There is a slight tremor to my hand as I take the receiver from her.

"Hi. This is Roxi Ingram," I say.

Carlo's deep, accented voice fills my ear. "Ah, bella. It has been much too long since we spoke."

I pause. Take a deep breath and collect myself.

"Hello, Mr. DeAngelo."

"Carlo," he corrects.

"Carlo," I say, and wait for my stomach to settle.

"I apologize I have not called you before. I have been very busy and I am on my way out of town again. I am wondering if I may bring Bacci to you for say two weeks."

"When?"

This may be the answer to a silent prayer. My calculator of a brain is already figuring out what two weeks of having Bacci means to me in terms of cold hard cash. I am also excited about seeing Mr. X again.

"Tomorrow, if you will permit me to come by."

Tomorrow. Tomorrow. My mind is already racing. How will I react when I see Carlo again? We talk some more and he agrees to come by early in the morning.

I walk into the room where Yvette is busy with her schedules. I place the phone back into its cradle.

Yvette looks up and raises an eyebrow.

"Another man you like. You are beaming," she says.

"A client. A very nice client," I respond. "That's all."

Meanwhile I am mentally comparing Carlo and Reed. Both are charming in very different ways. But I feel a special closeness with Reed. This comes about as a result of having slept with him.

I must get these men out of my head. I have a business in trouble and I need a plan. I think about another direction my business could possibly go in. Maybe it is time to reinvent my company or maybe find a niche market. Maybe I should target corporations or businesses rather than individuals. If I got contracts with an agreement to use Wife for Hire exclusively I could have it made. It is not the first time I have toyed with this idea but in the past something has held me back. However desperate times call for desperate measures, and I am determined to succeed.

I hear the mailman crunch up the steps and letters go shooting through the slot and onto my wooden floors. I need a distraction, something mindless to do so that I can process my feelings. I retrieve the mail and begin sorting through it. I am particularly interested in the envelope with the *par avion* sticker. It has to be from Lindsay. I set the stack of mostly junk mail down and rip the envelope open.

My eyes get all misty. I can smell my child on that stationery. Until now I don't realize just how much I miss her. Lindsay has sent me photos of her and a strange man standing or sitting in front of several prominent landmarks. There she is with the man at the Eiffel Tower. And there she is again with the same strange man strolling the Champs Elysée and entering the Louvre.

Her letter is straight and to the point. She has fallen in love with France and in love with Jacques, a photographer she has met, who by the way, is not black. Her modeling career is taking off and she may never come home.

This does not surprise me. Lindsay is a vibrant, alive young woman, passionate about life and passionate about love. Deep down I knew she would feel this way about Paris. Sad as I am, I am happy for her. She dares to do things others only dream of. I fold the letter back into its envelope and make a halfhearted attempt to glance at my other mail, which luckily holds nothing of importance.

I return to find Yvette. She is done with her schedules so I send her home for the day. I make one last attempt to contact Vance. What he's done is not right. He has followed in the steps of Kazoo, resigning without giving me notice.

When I am alone I pop a CD into the player. I look at Lindsay's pictures again but they only remind me of how alone I am. I suddenly long for my own mother and I make a long-overdue phone call. She is not home so I leave a message. My love life might be looking up but professionally everything is crumbling around me.

I consider going to the gym and dismiss that idea. I consider going over to Margot's and decide I can't deal with more drama. What I really need is a vacation, some time away from the rat race. I can't really afford it but it will help keep my head on straight.

Yes, I know it is crazy. My business is in the toilet and my funds are rapidly depleting. But sometimes you just have to say screw it, and do what you need to do for yourself. A change of environment will help me recharge.

I get on the Internet and start looking at packages to the Caribbean. Then I change my mind and start exploring the fares to Paris. Maybe I will go see Lindsay after all. I am back and forth betwixt and between when my cell phone rings.

"Hi, beautiful. How's your day?" Reed says.

"Sucky."

Reed is silent, taken aback by my response. I explain to him what's going on.

"What you need," he says, "is a change of scenery."

"Exactly." I tell him that I am thinking of taking a vacation.

"I'll go with you," he says. "Right about now someplace warm would be ideal. How about the Islands? My friend has a house on Barbados he'll let us use."

A house means no hotel cost and the Caribbean is close enough. I've been to Antigua and St. Lucia a long time ago. I loved it.

"Sounds tempting," I say. "I've never really been to Barbados, just transited once. It's a place on my to-go list."

"We'll iron out the particulars in person. I'll be there in a couple of hours."

Reed hangs up before I can say another word.

Although it is fairly cold I decide rather than stay inside and drive myself crazy I'll go for a run. Running always helps clear my head and put things in perspective.

I pound the pavement for a good forty-five minutes and come back winded but feeling a heck of a lot looser. Since I was out longer than expected I have to rush to get ready.

I am putting the final touches on my makeup when the doorbell rings. I give a quick glance in the mirror and race off to answer. Margot stands on my front step, car keys in hand.

"You're turned out," she says, eyeing me up and down. "Going somewhere?"

"I don't know," I answer truthfully.

"Well, you're pretty dressed up for staying in."

I explain about Reed coming out to Long Island.

"Well, let me not keep you. There's been a new development and I was hoping we could talk."

Conscious of how chilly it is outside, I hold the door open. "Come on in," I say, standing aside. "Reed's not here yet."

Margot follows me as I wander off to get us wine. She keeps fiddling with her earlobe and nibbling on her lower lip: all signs of agitation. With Margot this is nothing new. I wait until we are seated on the couch, glasses of wine in hand, before asking.

"So talk to me about this latest development."

"Earl left his woman," she says. "He says he wants us to get back together."

I try to keep my expression neutral. Margot needs a sounding board not my personal thoughts on this matter. "How do you feel about that?" I ask carefully. Meanwhile I am thinking Earl is one confused man. I am also thinking given the changes Earl has put Margot through how can she trust him again.

"Honestly, I don't know," Margot answers. "Here I am just starting to get interested in Theo and now here is Earl turning up the heat. I've always thought he is what I want but I'm afraid he'll hurt me again. I just can't go through the constant ups and downs with him. At the same time I want my kids back."

Margot had been a major mess when Earl took up with his assistant. I'd been up nights with her. It had taken hours of therapy and medication to get her somewhat stable. She was obsessed with Earl and heartbroken to lose her children. I am relieved that she is thinking about what Earl is offering and not allowing him to manipulate her like a puppet.

"It would be nice to have your kids back," I say, "but I imagine it will be tough for them." I am thinking those poor children are the ones who are going to suffer. There's got to be some fallout when their father can't decide which woman he wants or loves.

"I worry about them," Margot admits. "If I decide not to get back with Earl I may have to take him back to court and prove to the judge that I'm the best bet. That'll cost money."

"You know I'll help." My doorbell rings. "We'll talk tomorrow," I say, standing up. I hug her. "You'll make the right decision. I know you will."

Margot walks with me to the door. Reed is standing on the front steps in a black single-breasted wool coat, holding a wrapped package in one hand.

"Hi, sweetheart." He kisses me on the lips, and my knees almost buckle. "Who's this?"

I introduce him to Margot, who eyes him up and down. "Nice," she whispers. "Very nice. Don't let him get away."

She heads off to her car, and Reed and I stand there staring at each other. I am a little shy remembering the intimacies of last evening. I get warm all over thinking of his hands on my body, the musky smell of him, the growling noises that he makes when he's about to come.

Reed hands me the wrapped box. "I couldn't resist getting you this," he says.

I remember my manners and invite him in. I pour him a glass of wine and then I sit next to him and meticulously remove the wrapping. I already know it's a jewelry box and from a store that is notoriously pricey. I was not expecting this.

Reed is looking at me expectantly so I pop open the lid. I gasp. Nestled against blue satin is a silver charm bracelet with dangling hearts. It is both tasteful and expensive. I've seen it in the catalog.

"Reed," I say, "it's beautiful but I can't accept it. It's too soon."

As if I haven't spoken, he puts the bracelet around my wrist and fastens the clasps. Then he kisses me on the lips, long and deep. Our tongues intertwine and dance back and forth. My body is alive and pulsing. I am determined not to make this one of those relationships that's totally based on sex. I want so much more. I slip out of his grasp. He's breathing heavily.

"Let's talk about our vacation." I say. "What's Barbados like?"

Reed starts telling me about his friend's beach house. It sounds like quite the place and comes with a pool and workout facility. As he is describing a huge patio overlooking the ocean, his cell phone rings. He glances at the dial, frowns and stabs a button.

"I don't mind if you answer," I say, watching his face carefully.

His expression undergoes a subtle change. He seems a little tense. "This isn't someone I want to speak to," he says.

I remember the other phone calls and his seeming avoidance of them. I wonder what's really going on. What is he not telling me? Is there another woman?

I am not particularly threatened. Men will be men.

CHAPTER 18

Reed and I cook dinner together, then decide to walk off the calories. Our walk ends at the same coffee shop where we initially met. By then we are freezing. I have latte and Reed has tea. We share a dessert and set a firm date for our Barbados trip.

I will leave Yvette in charge for the few days that I am away. Hopefully by then business will have picked up. Holding hands, we walk six freezing blocks back to my house. I am hoping that Reed plans to spend the night. The memories of last evening's lovemaking are still fresh in my mind and I want to re-create the wonder and explore going there again.

Reed settles in on my couch and pulls me down next to him. He kisses my temples and then the sides of my face. His palms brush my breasts. I am instantly on fire.

"Roxi," he says, "I am so glad I met you."

"Me, too," I say in a husky voice.

We kiss again with intensity and fervor. Things heat up quickly after that. Clothing starts coming off and we need to go to my bedroom before things go any further.

"Let's go into my room," I say, tugging on Reed's hand.

"I thought you would never ask."

Inside my bedroom, Reed and I stand nude in front of my full-length mirror. His arm is draped around my waist and his chin rests on my head.

"Don't we look beautiful together?" he says.

We do. He is fit, toned and golden brown all over. I am honey melon and glowing because just being with him makes me feel beautiful. My hair has worked its way free and skims my shoulders. My lips are slightly swollen from his kisses and my nipples are taut.

Reed's fingers span my stomach. He begins tracing circles against my skin. I turn into him. My arms circle his neck and he kisses me again. His tongue outlines my clavicle and he presses into me. His touch makes me want to bolt out of my skin.

Reed scoops me up and deposits me on the bed. He gets on his haunches and begins to trail his tongue across my flesh. I am pulsating and wired. I am writhing and wanting him to fill me up. I am scratching and clawing at him and I am making noises that are foreign to me.

When Reed enters me I moan. When he begins

pumping in and out of me we fall into an easy rhythm. My eyes are wide-open. I am flushed and panting. Reed's muscles are tight, his eyes are glazed and he is doing his best to hold on to control. I apply pressure, fastening my legs around his back and riding him. He is plunging in and out of me and I am yelping and bucking. Our bodies are gyrating. I bite Reed's shoulder. He bites me back.

I feel him convulse and I am right with him. We hold each other tight, stare into each others' contorted faces and find sweet burning release.

Already I am halfway in love with this man. And I think he just might be in love with me.

Reed gets up early next morning to drive back to The City. My house feels empty after he leaves and that in and of itself is strange. I have gotten used to being single and having my own space. I remember Carlo is bringing Bacci to me. I am not sure how I feel about him anymore. Talk about being confused.

I race around trying to pick up my house. Yvette should be over at any moment, thank God. Today we will send out mass e-mails to our entire database thanking everyone for their support and reminding them of Wife for Hire's services. I am getting desperate, and just about willing to try everything. And I am considering taking a vacation to Barbados. I must be out of my mind.

I get dressed, taking special care with my appearance. It is still fairly early so I bring a cup of coffee with me and I boot up my computer. I check my business e-mails and am pleased to see a few customers I haven't heard from in a while are in need of services. The twenty-percent discount has brought them back.

In the midst of the business mail is another e-mail from Bette Beautiful. Curiosity forces me to click on the message. I frown as I read another convoluted set of ramblings. This time the message is not couched in a story. I am being told that I need to back off from this woman's man if I know what's good for me.

I am called a number of nasty, vulgar names. It is clear from the presentation and the writing that she is not very well educated and her maturity level is that of a sixteen-year-old. She doesn't mention the man's name but I am to assume it is Reed she means. Why would a professional man hook up with a low-life looser? This woman is so crass I can't imagine why Reed would find her attractive.

I remember Reed's hesitancy to answer his own phone. Must be an old relationship gone sour, I decide. But how does this woman know who I am? Whatever, I will not dignify her lewd and demeaning comments by responding. She is clearly not worth it. I am not, and will never be, a candidate for *The Jerry Springer Show*. I decide to save this message, too. I'll discuss this with Reed when the time is right. Meanwhile I'll keep my own counsel.

I blank my mind and move on. First I decide to cancel my membership with the dating service. I need to give this thing with Reed a chance. I take care of that and am in the midst of answering some customer queries when Yvette arrives.

"Tell me we have new customers," she says, setting down a cup of Starbucks in front of me.

"Just a few old ones returning."

"That's got to be a good thing. What would you like me to do today?"

I hand her a list of things Vance was supposed to have taken care of. "Is there anything on that list you think you could handle?"

She peruses the list and hands it back to me. "I can take care of the dog walking, and I can pick up the Taylors' dry cleaning and check references for the handyman the Steins want to hire. Will that help?"

"Of course it will." I give her a little hug. The other chores can be split between me and Margot. I give Yvette the address of the family whose dog needs walking and I hand her the key for their home. I always insist on an extra key. I'll need to get the other one back from Vance.

As Yvette is grabbing her coat and preparing to take off, the doorbell rings.

Yvette glances at me. "Want me to get it?"

"No, I will."

I open the door to Carlo, eyes hidden behind the usual dark glasses. Something inside me stirs. He is holding a carrier with Bacci in it. A black sedan is parked next to the curb. This time he is using a driver. He gives me a huge embrace, the cat swings precariously from its carrier. Then he kisses my cheek.

"It is so good to see you, bella," he says. "Someone has to be putting that glow on your lovely face."

"Staying busy will do that to you." I am conscious of him still standing on my front step, clouds of cold air coming from his mouth.

"Come in and have a cup of coffee with me," I offer.

Yvette nods and smiles at Carlo. He nods back and gives her a grin as if she might be an unexpected breakfast treat. With another wave and a seductive smile, she sidles by him, taking off to complete the duties she said she would do.

Carlo follows me into the kitchen, removes his coat and gloves and takes a seat at the counter. He lets Bacci out of his carrier and the cat promptly wraps herself around my ankles and nuzzles me with her nose.

I scratch Bacci behind the ear then I straighten and ask, "How do you take your coffee?"

"Black and sweet."

Easy enough. The pot is full, which means all I have to do is pour. I shake some biscotti from a tin and put them on one of my good plates. I set both before Carlo and then I sit down and join him.

"How is business?" he asks, blowing on his coffee.

"Awful. Things are very slow."

"Could be the time of year," he says knowingly. "You're running special offers I'm sure."

"I'm trying pretty much everything."

I don't want to sound despondent and desperate. Carlo is still my customer and while we have a good rapport, he doesn't need to hear my woes.

"What if my corporation uses Wife for Hire exclusively? Will that help?" he asks.

Help? It will save the day. I hope my eyes aren't bulging out of my head.

I go into business-owner mode. "Just what does *exclusively* mean?"

"Well, it means providing transportation for the executive staff of three of my companies. It means making hotel and airplane reservations for the same group, catering meetings, planning events, that kind of thing. I would put you on retainer."

Carlo names a figure he is willing to pay just to keep me available. This time my eyes do pop out of my head.

"Who's handling all of this right now for you?" I have the presence of mind to ask.

"The various assistants of various departments, and not very well. Most have their own responsibilities so a lot goes by the wayside. Interested?"

He doesn't have to ask me a third time. "Of course I am."

Carlo finishes his coffee and stands. "My attorney will send you a contract. You have your people look it over and if everything seems okay we are off and running."

"Thank you! Thank you!" I say.

I notice he hasn't haggled over pricing or asked for a corporate discount. He has just handed me an enormous gift at a time I needed it most. I can kiss this man, really kiss him.

Carlo stands, shrugs on his coat and tugs on his gloves. As he is leaving he turns to me. "Roxi have you given any thought to taking your company in a new direction?"

"What do you mean?" I ask carefully. I've never fooled myself into believing I know everything. Suggestions from a successful man who has clearly made it are much appreciated.

"Ever thought about upgrading your demographic? Taking your business up a notch?"

I remain silent, waiting for him to go on.

"In addition to what you're doing you could create a concierge service for people with no time but willing to pay premium prices. If you make your focus major corporations instead of individuals, you'll have it made. Corporations will pay big money to keep their executives happy. You could smooth the way for executives relocating. And you could even open franchises in some of the major cities. There's great software out there to help you with that."

We are on the same wavelength. My mind is already racing like crazy. I already have DeAngelo Creations business, and Carlo would give me excellent references. That should give me entrée into other major companies.

"That's great advice," I say, and then I act on my urge and kiss Carlo on the cheek.

Somehow, and I don't know how this happened, we kiss for real, and I am pressed up against his lean, hard body. My fantasy is alive. Kissing Carlo is something I have always dreamed of so I savor the moment. I am lost in the smell of damp wool and expensive cologne. I am lost in him. His kiss is everything I have dreamed of and more. I am beginning to think Reed who?

We separate and look at each other with something akin to wonder.

"I shouldn't have done that," Carlo said. "It was presumptuous of me."

"But very nice," I said surprising myself.

"We will talk when I get back."

With that he hurries off and I stand there awed by what has just happened. I wave him off. Then I touch my lips and think about his kiss and how it makes me feel.

Later I force myself to go about my business and try not to feel guilty about Reed. Instead I focus on the meeting I have set up with a disgruntled customer; a chronic complainer. Taiko Tanabe has been with me since the very beginning and pays her bills on time. So it is in my best interest to smooth her over.

I return to my computer and assign myself a list of chores Vance was supposed to have taken care of, like emptying a client's mailbox and making sure that tickets for a Giants game are purchased. I also have to go on the hunt for a particular beer that a client fell in love with on a recent business trip to Phoenix. I will do all of this after my meeting with Taiko.

While I am driving to JFK Airport where I have agreed to meet Taiko Tanabe, my client, I keep replaying my conversation with Carlo DeAngelo over and over again. At the same time I am trying to get his kiss out of my head. Lucky for me traffic on the Southern State and Belt is minimal. By the time I find a spot in short-term parking, I am excited and challenged by the idea of growing Wife for Hire. Already I am playing around with names for the new division.

Taiko is waiting for me at the bar of one of those trendy restaurants in the international terminal. She is more often out of the country than in. She has her own business coaching executives on social skills and protocol when doing business in foreign countries. She is a tiny woman, but do not let her size fool you. She is one tough cookie. And although she likes to complain, she pays me well so I put up with her.

I've already figured that Taiko will not keep return-ing if she is not satisfied. She isn't looking for freebies, either, she is just the quintessential perfectionist.

"Thank you for meeting me here," she says. Taiko is always gracious. "I will be training in Hong Kong and Tokyo for the next few weeks so it is important we get this straightened out."

I slide onto the bar stool next to her. "What seems to be the problem?"

Bottom line, she is unhappy with Vance.

"I do not think the cleaning service has been coming by regularly. My apartment was coated in dust when I returned. I asked that my refrigerator be stocked with specific items. It was not."

I apologize and tell her Vance is no longer with us. I assure her it will all be taken care of, and I tell her she will have a new person assigned that is more attuned to her needs. I have Yvette in mind. She and Taiko will probably be a better fit, anyway.

I pay for Taiko's two bottles of water and my cappuccino, because that is all she will let me do. She hands me a list of things she needs to have taken care of in her absence, and I assure her it will be done to her satisfaction. Then I get an idea.

"Wife for Hire is branching out," I say to Taiko.

"You are? What is it you are up to now?" She tosses back a lock of glossy black hair and fixes her heavily mascaraed eyes on me.

I do not break the stare. "We are starting a service geared to executives. People like you who don't have the time to run or maintain households. Executives recently relocated or just too busy to tend to everyday chores."

"This sounds like a good plan. You will need new employees then," Taiko says with brutal honesty. She is already one step ahead. She hands me her card. "I'd like to speak to you more when I get back. Given what I do and you do, we can work something out. Better start interviewing now, find people who are not errand runners but classy." She slides off her stool and picks up her hand luggage.

Our audience has ended. I feel good. Taiko is a potential second client. She might be tough as nails but she is respected in the industry. Now we are talking about global possibilities for Wife for Hire.

I leave JFK Airport on a high. I am euphoric as I complete the many mundane duties that require my time. I am also thinking Yvette may be the perfect spokesperson for this new venture. She has the looks to head up my concierge effort and she is very cosmopolitan. Businessmen will love her and she will have them eating out of her hand.

While I am at the post office getting a client's mail I check Wife for Hire's mailbox. As usual there is a huge stash of junk mail. I toss the majority in the garbage and scan the remainder. It seems I've acquired more new clients, and for that I am grateful. A couple of old ones are also back. I'm still not up to last year's total but things are beginning to look up. It would be nice to go on vacation worry free.

Amongst the reduced stack are a few personal pieces of correspondence. One in particular catches my eye because it is a red envelope and looks like an invitation.

I slit the envelope open and my stomach lurches.

On a plain white card are pasted these words:

"Slut. Find your own man and leave my husband alone!"

CHAPTER 19

My hand trembles a little as I hold the card and read it again. This couldn't be meant for me. I've always had a policy of not dating married men. Plus, the only man that I'm dating is Reed. I don't think he's anyone's husband. I've stayed over at his place and he's stayed over at mine. If there's a wife in the picture, she must be living elsewhere.

I think about the strange e-mails I've gotten in the past few days. I think about the phone calls and Reed's reluctance to answer. I wonder if he's living a double life. It looks as if I am going to have to have a conversation with him sooner rather than later. I tuck the card into my purse and take what's left of the stack out with me to the car. But this really has shaken me up. I hate messy situations.

I'd been planning to call Reed and share my good news with him, but now I don't know. Instead I decide to take a drive and clear my head. I somehow find myself driving to Long Beach.

Long Beach is the type of beach community that

comes alive in summer. My friend Sophia from my corporate days still lives here. She's single and has a partner. Sophia is one of these free-spirit types that totally believes in living in the moment. We get together maybe once a year, and in between we do some serious phone time.

I am on Sophia's street when I pull out my cell phone. Her car is parked in the driveway and that seems strange given it's a workday. It is short notice but I don't think she'll mind me popping in.

"Hey, girl," she says after a couple of rings. "What are you up to?"

"I'm in front of your town house. Feel like a visitor?"

Sophia lets loose with a throaty chuckle. "You're not a visitor, you're family. Bring your gorgeous self in."

I pull the Land Rover into Sophia's driveway and park next to her Bauxter. She is the kind of woman that makes an impression because she is larger than life and comfortable with it. Before I can push the buzzer the door opens up and Sophia stands before me, a hand on her hip. She looks me up and down.

"What's wrong?"

"Everything," I sniff. I can't stop the tears from falling.

I am scooped into her arms before I know it.

Sophia is one of those women who will never be thin and does not care to diet. She is busty and hippy and chooses clothes that camouflage everything. She is olive-skinned with black wavy hair pulled off her face to reveal high cheekbones. Sometimes she secures the masses of hair with chopsticks or other implements that none of us would consider using. The look works for Sophia and fits her dramatic personality. Men find her incredibly sexy and her partner adores her.

Although Sophia is working from home today, she is draped in an embroidered shawl, secured by a large silver pin on the shoulder. Her wide peasant skirt skims her ankles and the toes of her bare feet sport numerous silver rings.

She squeezes me against her again.

"So what brings you to see me, Mammy?"

"I was in the neighborhood," I say. "My car took on a life of its own."

I get another throaty chuckle. "Don't give me that. You've got man problems. We need to talk."

I can smell coffee coming from the kitchen and can really use a cup. Sophia stands aside to let me enter the room that she has turned into an office. Two monstrous computers blink at me. She is amazingly in tune.

"Coffee?" she asks when I am seated on one of her colorful beanbag chairs. Her place is retro and tastefully decorated.

"I'd love some."

Sophia returns with two steaming cups in hand and takes the beanbag chair opposite me. "So what's up?" she asks.

I explain to her what's happening. I tell her about the vague e-mails, Reed's phone calls and now this woman threatening me.

"Can you prove where they're coming from?"

"No. And I don't want to sound like a whining baby to Reed."

Sophia takes a sip of her coffee. "My advice to you, then, is to keep your mouth shut and your ears and eyes open."

"But what if he's married?"

"What if this isn't about Reed? What if it's about some woman's insane insecurity?" Sophia counters. "Wouldn't you feel stupid for having said anything? Your relationship is too new for you to start creating waves. Just play the wait-and-see game."

"It's because it's so new that I feel I need to say something," I whine. "If I don't set the tone now it will only get worse. What if he does have another woman in the picture?"

"How you handle yourself and him will determine the outcome," Sophia says. "I'd just chill."

I grunt something. I am not used to sitting back and waiting. I like to be able to chart the outcome.

Sophia gets up to top off both of our cups.

"If you feel you have to say something, at least wait until you get back from Barbados. You're spending five whole days with the guy and that should give you a better sense of him. How many married men can up and disappear for five days? See what happens while you're there. You'll be able to determine if you have one hundred percent of his attention."

I nod my head. Sophia has always given good advice. She once confided in me that she'd been stalked by another woman and had her car vandalized. She'd had no problem having the woman arrested.

All this drama is new to me and sets my teeth on edge. My philosophy has always been if a man no longer wants me, then I walk away. What's the point of hanging on after a man shuts down, and why even bother harassing the new woman? Scaring her off isn't going to do you good. He's already made his decision; a decision that doesn't include you.

Sophia fills me in on what's going on at my old workplace. Nothing new there. It is the usual corporate politics, sabotage, backstabbing and people hooking up. I don't at all miss it.

I feel so much better for having spoken with her. She doesn't mince words and her practical, down-to-earth advice is exactly what I needed. We hug, kiss and promise to get together more often. I leave, vowing to keep my mouth closed and my ears open.

Back home I call Yvette and tell her there's something I'd like to discuss with her. She invites me over to her house for dinner. I go, leaving my cell phone behind. I need a break from the real world intruding.

Yvette on such short notice serves up a spread that has my mouth watering.

She's made pasta and a salad. We have tomatoes and feta cheese as a side. The bread she serves is warm and crusty and we try a very nice bottle of wine. Afterward we sip on sweet, milky coffee. Jessica is, of course, nowhere to be found.

"I like this new idea of yours very much," Yvette says. "If you market it right there is quite a bit of money to be made."

"Actually I had new inspiration." I explain about Carlo.

"Regardless. Now, this is what I think we should do. We need to get ahold of a directory of all the Fortune 500 businesses in the area."

I nod my head. We are in tune, as I knew we would be. In a few short days we have become not just business associates but good buddies.

"We will design a very special and classy invitation to these companies. They must want to list with her.

We will appear exclusive as if we are picking and choosing who we want business from."

"I like the way you think," I say, with renewed enthusiasm. "In fact, so much I would like it if you headed up this new division."

Yvette's jaw practically hits the floor.

"You are pulling my leg. I am brand-new. What do I really know about running a business?"

"You have insight and vision," I say, clinking my glass of wine against hers and then impulsively adding, "I will be taking a short vacation next week to the islands and I am going to leave you in charge of the company and the cat. You will need to hire the right people for our venture so you may want to run an ad and start interviewing."

Yvette's eyes light up. "You are trusting me with your company. I am practically a stranger."

"For each new piece of business you bring in I will give you a nice commission."

"I love you," Yvette says, dancing around. "I will not let you down."

Yes, I know I am taking a chance on a new employee, but sometimes a person has to go with her gut. A burst of fresh energy might be just what I need to put my business back on track. I am counting on a change of scenery to get my groove back. In Barbados

I will relax and hopefully return refreshed and bursting with ideas.

I leave Yvette's feeling content and not just from her delicious food. I am going home to do an inventory of my closets. I am going to start packing for my trip to Barbados and I am going to call Margot and set up a girlfriends' day for us to go shopping. I'll treat for a manicure, pedicure and facial. Yvette can run the business that day.

I am feeling upbeat and energized. My new business venture is going to be a huge success and I'll be raking in money. I just know it.

Life is about to take a more positive turn. I can feel it.

Ten days later I am in Barbados at Reed's friend's very chi-chi villa in a resort. I am already three shades darker than when I left the States and I am guessing at least five pounds heavier. All Reed and I have done so far is eat and drink. We have downed copious amounts of rum punch and we have eaten flying fish and Johnny cakes, curried chicken and rice.

We are acting like a honeymoon couple. Reed can't seem to keep his hands off me and I have difficulty doing the same. During the day we lie in chaise lounges partially covered by a huge umbrella. We've tried all the water sports and now I've decided to catch up on my reading. I have a rattan bag I bought at a market, filled with novels from my favorite authors. I just love Michelle Monkou and Simona Taylor's work. Both are Caribbean women and can tell a good romance story.

I have left my laptop home. I do not want to think about work or a woman sending me threatening e-mails warning me to leave her husband alone. I am here to have fun and get to know Reed better.

He is over at the tiki bar getting us our standard rum punches. The staff at the resort is trying to convert us to rum and coconut water but I like my punch and so we stick to it.

"Hey, you," a young, buff Bajan man says to me in his unmistakable Caribbean accent.

He is coffee-colored and wearing swimming trunks that skim his knees. There is not an extra ounce of flesh on him anywhere.

I lower my sunglasses and smile at him. He is old enough to be my son. He is just being friendly I decide.

The boy-man takes my smile as a welcome. He plops down in Reed's vacated chair.

"Uh, that's taken."

"What's a lovely looking woman like you doing on paradise alone?" he asks.

Oh, gawd! He is hitting on me. "I'm not alone," I answer.

"Now, that's disappointing." Despite what I've said, he makes no attempt to leave. "What are you reading, luv?"

I show him the cover of Michelle's book. A man and a woman are in a clinch like you wouldn't believe. They really need to get themselves a hotel room.

"A romance novel," my new friend says. "Bet you wouldn't need to read dat if you were with me. I'm Brian, by the way."

"Nice to meet you, Brian." I do not offer my own name in return. I am not looking for trouble. I'm not Stella and I don't need my groove back. I have Reed who strokes my ego and the other places that are pulsing.

"And you are?" Brian prompts.

"Ms. Ingram," Reed says with an edge to his voice. He's come up behind us. "You're in my chair, by the way."

Brian doesn't seem that concerned but he slides off the lounger and flips a salute Reed's way.

"You shouldn't leave this lovely woman alone."

The two men eyeball each other. Neither seems willing to back down.

After a while Reed shakes out the crumpled towel Brian has just lain on and spreads it out again. He shoves his sunglasses on his nose and reaches across and takes my hand. Brian is still standing there.

Reed ignores him. "Nap time before dinner, doll."

"Okay by me."

I wiggle my fingers at Brian and he reluctantly takes off. When he is out of sight, Reed leans over and says to me.

"Robbing the cradle?"

I laugh. Good to keep him on his toes. "He's probably a couple of years older than Lindsay. Do you have a problem with that?"

"No one would believe you have a twelve-year-old much less a kid in college."

I thank him and squeeze his hand. "What about our nap?"

Reed immediately perks up quickly. "Bed is something I am always ready for." He wiggles his eyebrows at me and I swat him on the chest.

We gather our things and head for the villa that Reed's friend loaned us. I really like Reed and I'm maybe a few crazy beats away from falling in love. But I am still mindful that I may have competition and crazy competition at that.

Inside is airy, white and the air-conditioning is humming. We start stripping off clothing the moment the front door closes. A nude Reed is at the refrigerator fetching us drinks of punch. We have a good supply stocked. I go into the bedroom. The maid has been in and the four-poster bed sports crisp clean linens. It is shrouded by a mosquito net. I climb onto the bed and position a pillow under my hips. I am already thinking about what I want Reed to do to me and how I will pleasure him.

He comes in and carefully sets our glasses on the nightstand then joins me in bed. Reed's warm body covers mine and he begins kissing me, starting at the tip of my ears and moving down to nibble my toes. My body as usual is alive and every nerve wired.

I wrap my legs around Reed's butt. I draw him into me. I am already moist where it counts and I require minimal foreplay. I hear the waves lapping outside, and the sun coming through the skylight bathes us in a golden light. Our bodies adjust to a comfortable pattern and we are off on a ride of our own.

I am soaring, reacting, giving as good as I am getting. My toes curl and the keening I hear is mine. I reach the pinnacle and with Reed go hurling over the top. No one, but no one, has ever made me feel so alive and uninhibited. It's a nice feeling to soar.

Later, Reed and I have dinner in an old converted clapboard house with a wraparound porch and tiny backyard. The dining room holds seating for twenty and the menu has already been preplanned. Tonight being a Wednesday, conch chowder is being served.

For the entrée there is curried goat, rice and black-eyed peas served with a fresh salad.

Lit candles flicker making patterns against the ceiling and walls. On colorful batik mats are hollowed-out coconut shells that serve as plates. The room is scented by vases of fragrant frangipani.

Dessert is a pungent black rum cake and coconut ice cream that is supposedly hand churned. At the urging of the owner we try rum and coconut water but we both agree we still like our rum punch better.

All that rum leaves me a little bit drunk. I decide maybe it's best from now on to stick to iced water. Reed slaps down a credit card and we depart.

Outside he points to the half-moon overhead. "Let's walk and burn off some calories."

Liking the idea, I take off my shoes. I want to feel the sand underfoot and between my toes. Reed places an arm around my shoulders and we walk through the surf. I don't care that the hem of my dress is getting wet. I am enjoying just being with him.

It's day three and I haven't once called Yvette to see how the business is doing. I have sneaked a call in to Lindsay, though. How can I not call my baby? I want to check up on her and make sure that this new man isn't taking up all her time. I want to make sure that she is keeping her promise to me and that she'll be going to school.

We walk another ten minutes toward an old wooden pier we had spotted during an earlier journey. We sit for a while, our feet dangling but not quite touching the water. The moon disappears. Reed kisses me and I kiss him back and soon we are making out like crazy, which leads to us making love. I hope no one sees us.

It's a wild and crazy ride, made more passionate by the thought of discovery and the fantasies playing out in my head. I am on a Caribbean island with a man who is perfect. Too perfect.

When we are done we straighten our clothing and Reed helps me up. His breath is a soft whisper against my cheek.

"Roxi," he says, "we should talk about moving in together."

I glance at him, but now it is too dark to see his expression.

I am truly stunned. I wonder how we got here.

CHAPTER 20

I do not commit one way or the other. The next two days pass in a blur, more sunning and swimming, drinking and making love.

Back in New York I throw myself into the plans for expanding my business. I am pushing Reed off, not giving him an answer. Things are moving too quickly for me. I tell him I am thinking about his proposal.

Yvette has done a remarkable job in my absence. She has researched companies she thinks can use our business and she has designed these elegant burgundy-and-black e-vites that she plans to whiz through cyberspace.

"I've done something you may not approve of," she says when we are seated in my home office, sipping coffee and reviewing the schedule for the day.

"What's that?" I am somewhat distracted as I sort through my personal mail.

"I posed as a customer and made an appointment to see Service Not Incidental's operation. They don't know me from a hole in the wall so it was easy to go through the motions."

She now has my full attention.

"And what's the verdict? What do we need to be doing better?"

Yvette thinks about it for a moment. "Overall I was not impressed."

"But I've lost a lot of business to that outfit. They must be doing something right."

Yvette stands, stretching her long body. "They're a new outfit and they've undercut your prices. There are offices you can walk into, and yes, they are beautiful, this makes people feel more secure. They're not sending payments to a PO box or meeting you at a restaurant. They can sit down with a live person and talk to them about their needs. These women are clever enough to serve tea, coffee and biscuits— That's right Americans say *cookies*." Yvette shakes her head. "But the owners aren't sophisticated or polished, they're just eager to please."

"You're suggesting we need offices, then. That's a costly investment."

"If you shared space with another business it shouldn't be too bad. All you really need is one room."

I like it that Yvette is full of ideas. I place the blade of the letter opener under the flap of an envelope and say, "I'll have to investigate renting space. It may be a good idea, especially if we're taking the business in another direction. Now to come up with a swanky address and cheap."

"There are some new office buildings being constructed on Merrick," Yvette offers. "What about them?"

"I doubt they are in my price range."

"You might be surprised. From what I hear no one's beating the doors down to get into them. We should check them out. I heard they were offering incentives."

"Like what?" I ask.

"Like three months free rent, which would be perfect and would give us some time to get the money up."

"Okay, I'm in," I say excitedly.

I remove the letter from the envelope I'm holding and scan it quickly. A slew of hateful words rush out at me. I feel hot, flushed and bile rises in my throat.

You bitch. I warned you to leave my husband alone. He doesn't want a dried-up old spinster like you. He only took you to Barbados with him because you were easy. Forget about long-term plans. He's not free. I'll never let him go.
   The Wife!

If I had any doubt who she is referring to, I now know for sure. One mention of Barbados and that is it.

As upset as I am, I still see the humor in it. The woman who is writing these letters is desperate and unsure. She clearly doesn't know what a spinster is. Either that, or she's making an assumption that I've never been married and in the same position as she. It's kind of pathetic.

I am seeing Reed later this evening and this conversation is long overdue. I hadn't wanted to ruin our vacation. But now I need to know what I am up against. I hope he is not married, and even if he's separated, it makes me uneasy that he would be on an Internet dating site and reaching out to unsuspecting women. What kind of decent man does that?

"Is everything okay?" Yvette asked. "Can I get you some water?" She is standing there staring at me.

The room sways and then rights itself. My forehead is moist and my hands clammy.

"I'll be fine," I say, tucking the letter back into its envelope with shaking hands. "Some woman thinks I'm after her man. The hazards of dating, I suppose. Are you dating anyone?"

Yvette shakes her head. "Not much to date out there. The whole process is frustrating so I'm better off staying home. Men are such cowards and insensitive at times."

"I hear you." I leave it at that. Yvette does not need more specifics and since I don't quite know what I am dealing with, why pull her in?

Now I'm anxious to see Reed. And frankly I am angry with him for withholding information and getting me involved in something this sordid. This person is over the top and as far as I am concerned a little bit off.

Yvette picks up on my desire to be alone.

"I'm going to take off unless you need me for something else?" she says. "Jessica is on a sleepover and I relish the few hours of peace and quiet."

I thank her and send her on her way home. So far she is earning every dime of the pittance I am paying her.

I dress carefully and think about how I am going to handle this. What it may come down to is me getting into bitch mode. I'd prefer not to be confrontational. I need to be able to hear Reed's side of the story if there is a side of the story.

Again I think why would Reed hook up with a loony toon? It makes me wonder if his relationship with me is all an act. Dysfunction after all tends to attract dysfunction.

I decide to drive into the city. I park my car in public parking, taking advantage of the overnight rates and walk the two long blocks to Reed's place. It is cold and I huddle into my lined leather coat, playing out different ways to broach the conversation.

His doorman nods at me and doesn't ask whom I'm visiting. This is a good sign, I think. He's getting used to me. Reed and I have talked earlier and we both agreed that this is a stay-at-home night. We plan to cook together and try a new bottle of wine.

Since we are not yet at the stage where I have his key, I press the buzzer and wait.

The door is flung open and a delicious smell wafts its way out into the hallway. I am scooped up into Reed's arms and given a passionate kiss.

"Something smells wonderful," I say when I am able to talk.

"You smell wonderful." He turns me this way and that. "New coat?"

"Old as the hills."

"You'd never guess. Why are we standing out here in the hallway?"

I am whisked inside. I hand Reed my leather coat. He lets out a low wolf whistle. I am wearing butt-hugging jeans and a V-necked sweater that shows a hint of cleavage. I have on black ankle boots with three-inch heels.

I shake a warning finger at him. "You promised to feed me. We were supposed to cook together."

"I am feeding you. Everything's already started."

I go into the kitchen and peer into his pots. He's got

a sauce with a tangy aroma going. He has shrimp almost the size of my fist on a low flame. There are mushrooms and tomatoes sautéing. The man's a gourmet.

"What's there left to do?" I ask.

"Pour wine and keep me company." Reed gives me another heart-stopping kiss.

I refuse to be distracted. I came here with a purpose. Before we have dinner and end up in bed we need to have our talk.

I find the white wine in the refrigerator and pour us both a glass. On the kitchen counter are pâté, cheese and a loaf of crusty bread. Reed tastes his sauce and begins kissing the back of my neck.

"Uh-uh," I say, stepping away. I walk toward the window and look down at the East River. I hear him come up behind me. His arms go around my waist and I feel the heat coming off his body.

"Something's up, hon. What is it?"

Careful not to spill my glass of wine, I turn into him. I decide the only way to approach this is to be direct and gauge his reaction.

"Do you have a wife?" I ask.

"What?"

"The answer is either yes or no."

"Not anymore." A muscle jumps in his cheek.

I am directly in his face now. "What does *not anymore* mean?"

"I'm in the process of a divorce."

"How long has this been going on and why didn't you tell me?"

"Would it have made a difference?" he says, his voice low.

"Damn straight it would. I don't get involved with married men."

I am angry now. How dare he be so cavalier? He's had ample time to mention this but never has. I've been sleeping with this man. I went away with him. I am steps away from falling in love with him and I am getting threatening e-mails and letters from his wife. A wife I have never heard of until now. This is the first he's told me he's in the process of getting divorced.

And he's the one who initially contacted me. This woman, this lowlife with the foul mouth and screwed up thinking, blames me for ruining her marriage. How many other innocent women has this man deceived?

My head is spinning from the news and I am still digesting it. I am involved with a married man; something I swore I never would do. I am wondering if there are more of us out there; unsuspecting women who think we've met the man of our dreams then later find out he's not free.

Reed is a woman's dream. He's a professional black male with a condo on the Eastside. His manners are exemplary and he's courteous and attentive. It figures he's too good to be true.

"Roxi," Reed says, "by now you must know I love you."

I hear the words but rationalize them as coming from a man caught in a lie and desperate to make everything right. He's never come right out and said he loved me before.

"How long since you and your wife have separated?" I get out in an unsteady voice. I will not cry.

"We made the decision to divorce almost a year ago."

That still doesn't answer my question. "How long since you haven't lived together?" I ask. He hesitates for a moment and I get completely in his face. "How long, Reed?"

"A long time."

"What's a long time?"

"Long enough."

I never could stand evasive behavior. It makes me crazy. I like people being straight with me and I am not into game playing. Despite what we shared I can no longer trust this man.

Needing to calm down, I start making circles around the room. Reed follows behind me.

"Roxi, as far as I'm concerned it's done with. My divorce papers are filed."

"That's the problem, as far as you are concerned. What about me? It takes two to have a relationship. And you said nothing. This whole thing came at me as a surprise."

I see a visible reaction. The muscles at the side of his jaw are jumping like crazy.

The acrid smell of smoke fills the air. Our food is on fire. Reed dashes toward the kitchen to turn off the burners.

He returns and grasps me by the shoulders. I step out of his reach.

"Your wife," I say through clenched teeth, "is sending me vicious e-mails and letters."

He blinks once, twice, and seems truly stunned.

"What do you mean?"

"Somehow she's gotten hold of my e-mail address. How is that possible? How does she even know about me?"

Reed thinks about that. "There was a time I moved out of the apartment and left my laptop here. She may have had someone hack into it."

I look at him, speechless. He has just incriminated himself. What that implies is that they were still very actively involved with each other up until recently.

"Then obviously she didn't trust you," I say.

I am furious now, my mind in a dozen different places at once. We are going around in circles and my illusions are already shattered. All I want to do now is get away from him. I storm off and begin pulling closet doors open.

"What are you looking for?"

"My coat."

"Oh, come on, Roxi. You're overreacting." He sounds exasperated and that just makes me more furious. I find my leather coat and shove myself into it. At the same time Reed is trying to peel me out of it. I belt my coat and look around for my purse. It is on the kitchen counter where I left it. I grab the straps and head for the door.

"What about dinner?" Reed shouts, tugging on the straps of my purse.

"You eat it," I say, and whisk myself out the door, slamming it in his face. I catch the elevator and quickly hop on. It is not until I cross the lobby and see the doorman's expression that I realize tears are streaming down my face.

I am hurting big-time. I feel as if someone has stuck a knife in my chest and twisted it.

I will never ever trust another man again, I swear.

CHAPTER 21

"So what do you think?" Shirley, the real estate agent, an ageing blonde who's been face-lifted a time or two, almost beyond recognition, asks.

Yvette and I exchange looks. The suite, although not especially large, faces Merrick Road. Glass doors lead out to a tiny balcony. If we want to lease we will receive three months free rent. All things considered it sounds like an awfully good deal to me.

"I don't know," I hedge. "I'm not sure it's large enough."

The blonde's manicured fingers splay. "You need the space to make an impression?"

"No, we need an area where there's a waiting room. Clients need to remain outside while we conduct our business inside."

The agent taps her chin with her fingers. "You could get one of those lovely folded screens and separate the room."

"That doesn't take care of sound," Yvette interjects.

"Well, there is one other suite that might work. It's a bit more expensive," she warns.

My cell phone is ringing like crazy. Reed again. I ignore it. I don't want to speak to him. We have nothing to say to each other. Besides, it's been days. I stab the mute button.

"Same deal? Same three free months rent?" Yvette is asking what I should be asking.

"Yes, and on a higher floor."

I don't care whether it is in the nosebleed area. Haggling with the agent has taken my mind off my troubles. For the past three days I've been dragging around with my lip on the floor. To add to my dismay, it is Alexandra who comes to pick up Bacci and not Carlo.

We follow the blonde up the elevator and into a suite with glass double doors. I envision all that smoked glass with WFH emblazed on it. There is a small waiting area and a larger inner room. There is a bathroom off to the side and there are French doors leading out to a larger balcony.

Yvette and I exchange looks. This is it. Exactly what we are looking for. But we don't want to appear too anxious. And we still haven't heard what the rent is.

"This might work," I say. I start walking around though the space is empty. I make tsking little sounds as if unsure. "I wonder if this waiting area will take a couch, it's kind of small."

"And there's barely enough room for two desks," Yvette adds, picking up on where I'm going with this.

"I might be able to do something about the rent," Shirley, the real estate agent, quickly adds. "Just let me make a few calls."

She gets out a cell phone and though it is frigid goes out to the balcony.

Yvette and I both cross our fingers while waiting for her to come back.

"It's a steal," I hiss.

"That it is. And with the three months leeway, making the rent shouldn't be difficult."

My cell phone rings. I glance at the dial to see Margot's number pop up. It's been a few days since we last spoke, highly unusual for us. But given her situation, I didn't want to burden her with my problems. She has her own.

"I've got to get this," I say to Yvette. She nods and goes out into the waiting area.

"How long have we been friends?" Margot demands the minute I pick up.

I sigh exasperatedly. "Quite a few years. Why the attitude?"

"Because you're dumping me for a new friend."

Margot is sounding like a jilted lover.

"I'm in no mood for drama, Margot," I say. "I've lived enough drama these last few days to last a lifetime."

"What's going on?"

"It's a long story. What's happening with you? What did you decide to do about Earl?"

She snorts. "I'll come over and tell you in person."

I explain that I am not home. Then I relent and agree to meet Margot at the gym later. She is, after all, my friend. We have been to hell and back together. After we work out we'll go to dinner and talk.

Shirley comes back in from the outdoors bringing the frigid air with her. Yvette returns from wherever she's wandered off to.

"I've just spoken to my boss," Shirley says. "If we can come to some agreement today, he'll knock another hundred dollars off the price."

I would be stupid to turn down such a good deal. But I hem and haw, anyway.

"Look," Shirley pleads, "we need to get these suites rented. You won't pay a penny for your first four months. That's about the best I can do."

I catch Yvette's eye. "We'll take it," I say. I have just gotten an extra month's cushion. "When can we move in?"

"We go back to my office. You give me a check, and I hand you a key."

And like that it is done. The entire transaction including credit check takes less than half an hour.

Outside, Yvette and I hug each other and scream.

"You did it!" she says.

"We did it!"

It's the first time since my devastating discovery about Reed's marital status that I feel elated about anything.

Without saying another word, Yvette and I head over to our new workspace.

Later, after a rigorous aerobic workout, Margot and I have a quick bite at a local eatery.

"You've been spacey and you've got this sad look in your eyes," she says, picking up on me. "Something wrong?"

At least she's not so wrapped up in her own woes that she doesn't notice. She's chain smoking again. I can smell it on her clothes. I take a bite of my tuna sandwich and set it back on my plate.

"I'm going to have to let Reed go," I say.

She eyes me suspiciously. "Why?"

I explain about him being married and about the threats I am getting from the soon-to-be-ex who doesn't want to let go.

"I don't know if I'd be so quick to walk away," Margot says. She's always had a different perspective on these things than I have. Look at her relationship with her own ex-husband.

"He's deceitful," I say. "And weak. He can't seem to control her. Makes me wonder what else I don't know."

"But there are lots of other things about him that you like." Margot looks at me as if I'm losing it. She just doesn't get it.

"True."

"You said he is attentive, caring, makes you feel like a million bucks. He takes care of business in the sex department, is solvent, good-looking, what the heck more do you want?"

I take another bite of sandwich. "I want a man who is free to pursue a relationship. I want someone who isn't going through a divorce with roller-coaster emotions. I don't want a man on the rebound or one in the midst of a messy divorce."

"And you think some of these supposedly single guys are that stable and together? My philosophy is capture him while he's still vulnerable and before he's back out on the market," Margot says sagely.

I decide I don't want to talk about Reed. It's much too painful. I'd had such high hopes for us.

"What did you decide to do about Earl?" I ask.

"I don't know. He's back with a vengeance and won't even give me space to think."

Par for the course. He can smell another man's interest. But even though I'm thinking this, I wisely keep my mouth shut.

We talk about my business and the new direction it's heading in. I tell Margot about the office space I've just rented.

"That's awesome, Roxi," she says, "and long overdue."

"I'll need your help."

"You know you can count on me."

I explain that I will need her to help me take care of things until a full complement of people are hired. I give her a hug.

"No one can replace you, ever," I say. "You're my bud."

There are tears in Margot's eyes. We've both been through tough times and we've always been there for each other.

My cell phone rings making me jump. Reed's number pops up. He doesn't seem to want to give it up, and I still can't bring myself to talk to him. Eventually voice mail will kick in.

We leave in separate cars and head back to our

separate homes. Life will go on. With time I will heal. I am a survivor after all.

When I pull into my driveway my instincts are to pull out again. A man is on my front steps, and that man looks suspiciously like Reed.

I sit for a while and keep the car's lights on. The muffled tones of a phone ringing come at me and I scramble through my purse.

"It's me," Reed says. "It's safe to get out."

Not in my book it isn't. I do not want him at my home at this hour of night. I've had a big day and right now confrontation is the last thing I want, yet I reluctantly slide out of the front seat. I can't risk a scene.

Reed meets me in the driveway.

"We need to talk," he says, taking my arm.

I try to pull away. "We've already spoken."

"Something else has come up. It's serious."

I toss a dubious look at him that's wasted in the darkness. A spotlight over my front door illuminates the shadows. I need to get there.

The driveway is not a good place to have this conversation anyway. If I lose my temper and begin shouting, my neighbors don't need to witness the show.

"You might as well come in," I say ungraciously as we climb my front steps together.

There's a light on in the living room, and I gesture

toward the sofa. If I don't offer him a drink or something to eat, maybe he'll leave shortly.

Reed takes a seat, legs splayed, arms hanging between his legs, head down. He is having a hard time looking at me. Oh, well, he should have thought about the consequences before he put himself out on the Web.

"What brings you all the way out here?" I ask when the silence stretches out.

"I'm in trouble."

I nod, thinking that's the understatement of the century. "You can say that again." I remain standing, hoping he will get the hint.

Reed looks at me with liquid eyes. "Look, I wanted you to know I might be doing some jail time."

"What do you mean, jail time?"

He's got my full attention now, and I don't like what I am hearing. Again, I feel as if I'm auditioning for *The Jerry Springer Show*.

Reed's hands cup his forehead. "I could kick myself for not being upfront with you."

"Why would you be doing jail time?" I ask, curiosity getting the better of me.

Seconds turn into minutes and he still doesn't respond.

"Let me be straight with you," he finally says.

"It's about time."

"When I asked my soon-to-be-ex for a divorce she turned ugly."

"That's a big surprise. I got the e-mails, the notes, remember?"

"She demanded money to go away, and when I refused, she filed a report with the police stating that I threatened her life."

This is starting to sound like a bad novel. They say truth is stranger than fiction.

"So were the police involved?"

"Not the first time."

"There was a second?"

Oh, gawd, this was worse than any talk show.

"Yes. She told them I threatened her with a bow and arrow."

I look at this man, this poster child for buppiehood dressed in chinos, loafers and cashmere sweater, and think, boy is my judgment off. I don't know what to say.

"They carted me away, handcuffs and all. Can you imagine the embarrassment?"

"So that's why I haven't heard from you in several days."

Dazed, he nods his head. He seems unable to believe this has happened. "Luckily I had a credit card and checkbook on me. That's the only reason I was able to bail myself out," he says.

I still don't know what to say. What's more, I don't know why he's telling me all of this. He's lied to me from the very beginning. And I no longer feel the way I did about him. He's lost my trust. I am more mad at myself than him.

"What happens now?" I eventually ask.

He shrugs. "I've hired an attorney. It's going to cost me a bundle to defend myself. She's claiming I was abusive all along."

"I'm sorry." I really am sorry for him but at the same time I am wondering if there is a kernel of truth to his wife's claim. It's not as if I've known this man for years.

"She's in a shelter for abused women somewhere," Reed rambles. "And she's got one of those feminist lawyers representing her."

"Why would she accuse you of something you didn't do?" I ask. "What would be the purpose?"

"Money. This all comes down to money."

"I don't understand."

Reed stands and stretches his arms. He rotates his neck to get the kinks out. I can tell he is stressed.

"She says I owe her for the three years we were married."

"Isn't New York a fifty-fifty state?"

Reed visibly balks. "I had assets way before she was in the picture. She brought nothing to the relationship."

Nice guy. I don't need to know this. The whole thing is sounding more bizarre by the minute. Why would Reed take up with an unhealthy woman unless there is something in it for him? Sex? Housekeeping services? Maybe a need to control?.

"Just be grateful you didn't have children," I say.

"I would never let that happen."

Deep down I know I should be more compassionate, but truthfully the whole thing bites. It's hard for me to get past the fact that he's lied to me.

"What I'm really here to say is that I'm sorry I dragged you into this mess," Reed says, playing his ace card.

"I'm sorry, too."

I stand. Reed comes closer. I step back.

"I really do care for you, Roxi," he says.

"Caring isn't enough."

I cross to the front door and yank it open. A frigid breeze blows in. There are tears in my eyes for all the things that could have been. I blink them back.

"Goodbye, Reed."

He looks at me solemnly and takes a hesitant step.

"Goodbye for now. This isn't over."

When he's gone I press my back against the closed door and allow myself a good cry.

I'd had such hope for us.

CHAPTER 22

Three weeks go by, and each day Reed's duplicity begins to hurt less. I throw myself into work and focus. There's enough on my plate to keep me busy. I'm relying on my marketing consultant to help me launch the campaign for this new aspect of my business. I am using my loan to pay for promotions. This Sunday there will be a huge ad in *Newsday*.

Yvette is working as diligently as me, although most of the time she spends at home on her computer. Jessica, her daughter, the terror of the neighborhood, needs reining in. Yvette researches new businesses to target, and we spend a portion of each day checking out thrift shops for furniture for the suite. Even Margot is pitching in and helping me do errands that would normally be assigned to Vance.

I haven't heard from Carlo in some time but assume he's back in the United States. Since Bacci was picked up by Alexandra I haven't heard the first word from him. I need to thank him properly. He gave me a running start to get this concierge business off the ground.

I also need him to sign contracts agreeing to use my services exclusively.

I pick up the phone and punch in a number.

"I need you to send a gift basket," I say to the proprietor who is a friend of mine.

"Where to?"

I give her DeAngelo Creations' address.

"What should the card say?"

"'Thank you for your idea. I'll call to set up an appointment to discuss the details of our collaboration. Best, Roxanne Ingram.'"

"Okay, I'll get it out today."

I hang up and decide to take a trip over to my new office. I still can't believe I am finally operating out of a real building. Every once in a while I pinch myself, and when I'm not pinching myself I indulge in a few sad moments. I miss Reed. Actually, I miss the idea of him.

I walk around the inside admiring the comfortable chairs in the waiting room and the painting hanging over the couch Yvette and I bought from a thrift store. We are still looking for desks with rich woods and an antique look to them. We're also on the hunt for a nice throw rug to warm things up.

A cappuccino and espresso maker would be perfect in one corner. Maybe I can buy one secondhand. I sit in one of the leather office chairs and swivel. I think about what I will do once the money really starts rolling in. Number one on my list is a trip to Paris to see Lindsay.

My phone rings. It is Yvette. She needs me to put out a fire. Somebody's kid was to have been picked up from school and the frantic mother and teacher are calling. This was to have been Vance's job. I must have dropped the ball when I was transferring assignments and missed this one. Lucky for me the school is only about ten minutes away. I race off.

Later, after I have apologized to the upset mom, removed the charge off her bill and offered another free pickup, I go home to put up my feet. I take a long slow soak in the tub, wrap myself in one of those huge terry cloth bathrobes and sit in front of the television set. I am close to nodding off when my cell phone rings. It is late. I am tempted not to answer, but something urges me to pick up.

"Bella. Carlo here. Sorry for calling so late."

I feel the old familiar flutter deep in my gut, and my tongue twists into a double loop.

"Roxanne, are you there?"

"I'm here."

"Did I wake you?"

"No, not at all. You caught me off guard. Normally I don't answer my cell after a certain hour."

"I am calling to thank you for the lovely gourmet basket," Carlo says. "It was unexpected, unnecessary and very much appreciated. I am also hoping we can set up a date."

Date as in he and I? I get another flutter.

"Send me a copy of your contract. I'll look it over, sign and we'll discuss it over dinner," Carlo says.

"I'll get one out to Alexandra. How is Bacci by the way?"

"Doing very well. And by the way, you will not be dealing with Alexandra on this matter. You and I will be speaking directly unless I am out of town. I trust that should not be a problem."

"No problem at all. In fact, I like that."

We talk some more. I agree to e-mail a contract to him, and Carlo promises to call back with a date and time to meet. Before he hangs up he says, "Pick a restaurant, bella, a very nice one, and I will take you out to eat."

This is what I have wanted for a long time and fantasized about forever. Yet I wonder if Carlo's interest is merely professional and I am making too much of this. Then I think of having his total attention for the minimum of a couple of hours, and staring into those soulful caramel-colored eyes of his.

I drift off to sleep thinking about Carlo. I think

about his beautiful chiseled face and smooth olive complexion. I think about his seductive lips. Maybe I am getting over Reed finally, or maybe he was just a passing fantasy; a distraction of sorts. Maybe my heart has always been with Carlo.

On Sunday I search *Newsday* and find my ad. I am happy with the end product. Even I would want to sign up for Other Options, as I've decided to call my concierge business. The remainder of the week I hold my breath as calls slowly come trickling in. Then on Thursday we get slammed, and phones ring off the hook. Everyone has questions about this new business and many sign up.

"Yes!" Yvette says, arms pumping above her head doing a war dance, as the phones continue to ring. "Yes!"

We are booking appointments like crazy. Before I know it she and I have two solid weeks booked. The companies that are calling are some of the more prominent. They vary in size and structure, and so do their needs.

I explain about the retainer they will need to pay and the contract they must sign. None of them seem overly concerned with my request.

I am seeing Carlo to discuss our contract tomorrow. We'll meet at a restaurant on the North Shore of Long Island. Margot is still seeing Theo, the doctor, and trying to decide whether to give Earl one last shot. She'll do just about anything to have her children back and I guess I can't blame her. She and I have agreed to meet for pedicures at one of those tiny Asian places that are all over New York. Afterward she is coming to my house to help me pick out something to wear.

When we are soaking our feet and enjoying an invigorating neck and shoulder massage, Margot says, "You're handling this whole business with Reed really well. I'd be throwing a hissy fit."

"I'm trying my best to move on."

The pedicurist towel dries Margot's feet and she wiggles her toes. "Ever thought about checking to see if Reed's still out on the dating site?"

I grunt. "Why would I do that? It's over."

"Curiosity. You might want to confirm whether he's a player or not."

"I don't care. Too much energy."

Margot nods her head knowingly. "Well, I do. That hound dog needs to be stopped. Give me his stats and I'll check him out when we get home."

I'm thinking I'd have to be a masochist to go poking around. But at the same time I am curious. I hate being played.

Two hours later my bedroom looks like the storage room of a department store. Heaps of clothing are on the bed, as well as every available surface. Margot and I have narrowed it down to two outfits. She thinks I should show a little leg, but I am of the mindset to play it safe. Even so, I'm considering a body-hugging dress that stops short of the knee and comes with a matching shawl. Truthfully, though, I'm leaning toward the other: a slim skirt with a matching jacket under which I will wear a camisole and pearls.

As I am mentally going through my accessories, Margot flips my laptop on.

"What site did you find Reed on?" she asks. "You know his stats, age, height, education, right? What's his screen name?"

I tell her what I know. She does a quick search and says, "Looks like he canceled membership on this site. I'm going to try another."

I leave the room to take care of a couple of things and come back with two glasses of water.

"Bingo! Look who I found," Margot says, tapping a nail against Reed's photo.

My eyes almost pop out of my head. The photo is one we had taken in Barbados together except he's cropped me out of the shot. To say I am speechless, hurt and feeling as if I have been played big-time is an understatement. Margot clicks an arrow, and the next photo pops up. This one is of Reed and Guinness. He's using that lovable dog as bait to reel women in.

I feel my eyes mist up and blink back tears.

"Let's see what the bastard has to say," Margot says, clicking on his profile.

Now I can barely see and there is a roaring in my ears that makes it impossible for me to hear. Margot is reading about Reed's search for the love of his life and about how much he wants to give this person his heart. He says he wants to design a house just for the two of them. Puhleese! It's the same kind of bologna he told me. Some other trusting woman will fall for his smooth charm. And the bugger has the nerve to list himself as "single."

Now I am really mad at myself.

"Please stop torturing me," I say to Margot. "I've been a sucker. I made a bad choice. Lesson learned."

"What an SOB," Margot says before muttering something really crude and vulgar. "Let's see how he operates with other women?"

"What do you mean?"

"Let's fix this player's wagon."

She begins typing and I quickly see what she's doing.

"You're creating a fictitious profile," I say. "What are you going to use for a photo?"

I am starting to panic. I have never done anything this wicked before.

"That part is easy," Margot says. "Hand me that

magazine. Now, let's see, there's got to be a certain type your boy goes for."

I hand over a copy of a popular African-American magazine and point out a few pictures that might work. Margot flips through the pages, picks out a polished-looking African-American woman with sparkling brown eyes and a wide smile, and says, "That's her. That's Savannah."

"She looks friendly and not the least bit threatening. Reed should like her," I say, quickly figuring out what Margot is up to.

Margot scans the photo and uploads it. She uses her own credit card to pay for the membership.

"There. Done. This is Savannah."

We both laugh. Laughing feels good.

"Now what?" I ask. My heart is palpitating like crazy.

"Now we get busy." Margot has a lot of experience tracking down players. She used to tail Earl, and she even knows how to access his cell-phone records, that's how she found out he was cheating on her. But that's another story for another day. Margot is already busy typing away.

"You're going to get us caught," I say, hanging over her shoulder and reading what she's just written. She hits the send button as I am digesting what she wrote.

So how do I meet a hot guy like you?

"Jeeze, Margot," I say, "talk about being Ms. Subtle?"

"Straightforward pays. That way there's no mis-understanding and we find out if he's a hound dog."

"No good will come of this," I mutter under my breath.

"Closure will come of this," Margot says, wisely. "Something I never got with Earl. It's not like he's the love of your life or anything. He was just a diversion. You wanted it to work because you wanted to get your mind off that client of yours."

Margot, neurotic as she can be, knows me better than even my own mother. She is right. I wanted to fall in love with Reed, needed to. Carlo DeAngelo seemed out of my league, and after Max, well, I needed a salve for my ego.

Carlo is my dream man but Reed seemed more at-tainable. He is single, professional, without child and seemed interested in me.

I wonder how many me's there are out there. Wom-en who've fallen for Reed's seeming sincerity; vul-nerable women who've thought he was for real and in return had had their hearts broken.

Now I don't feel one bit bad about posting a fake profile. Let's see how long it takes for him to respond to Savannah.

I high-five Margot, and we go off to have a glass of wine.

CHAPTER 23

"Can I help you, madam?" The affable maître d' asks the minute the valet takes off with my car.

"I have reservations." I give him my name.

The restaurant where Carlo and I are meeting will never make the A list. But it does have excellent seafood and impeccable service. It also has private booths. He and I will be able to conduct a conversation without shouting at each other.

Carlo had offered to come and get me, but I insisted that we meet here. I am more cautious these days, and since I'd been running around all day, I needed the time and space to get dressed leisurely. Driving my own car says I'm in control. Can you tell I've developed major trust issues since Reed?

The maître d's attention is now elsewhere. He is bobbing his head and grinning as guests enter and leave. I am clutching the envelope with the contracts and waiting to be seated. Finally he turns me over to a hostess—a tall thin woman who could have been a model in her heyday.

"Ms. Ingram?" Her smile is wide, friendly. My guess is the name DeAngelo means something to her. "Mr. DeAngelo is already seated. I'll take you to him."

I check my coat and we bypass a number of waiting people, those without reservations perhaps.

Carlo has reserved a corner booth for us. A huge window serving as a backdrop looks out on the lake. The water is iced over, and spotlights shine onto a glassy surface where several people are attempting to skate. Music comes from another room, and I catch glimpses of people dancing.

Always the gentleman, Carlo glides out of his booth. He is wearing a dark suit and white shirt open at the collar. He looks hotter than hot. His curly dark hair lies in flat ringlets against his head and is still damp. His eyes light up when he greets me. And I feel that old familiar thing happen as my body goes numb.

"You are stunning, bella."

"Thank you."

I sit across from him thinking how glad I am that I chose the more conservative outfit. A bottle of wine waits in a nearby bucket. We are handed menus and the waiter pours our wine.

"Salud," Carlo says when the waiter leaves.

"Cheers." I clink my glass against his. "Shall we discuss business before or after dinner?"

"Before. That way we will have the entire meal to talk about other things."

Is he coming on to me? I still don't know. I smile, nod in agreement and slide the envelope with his contracts over to him. Carlo takes them out of the envelope and peruses them carefully. He pulls out a Mont Blanc and with a flourish, signs all three copies before slipping one into a monogrammed black briefcase. He hands the other two back to me.

"So how are you really doing, Roxi?" he asks.

"I'm feeling good about life in general. Thanks to you, my business is back on its way up and I feel ready to take on the world."

"You do not need to thank me," Carlo says. "You are a bright woman. You would have figured things out yourself."

I am jittery inside but manage to smile at him.

"You gave me my start. That's an enormous leap of faith to take with someone you barely know."

He flicks an imaginary speck of something off the cuff of his shirt and looks at me. "My instincts are usually pretty right on. That's how I've built successful businesses. And that's why one of my foundations creates dreams. We are similar to Make a Wish."

Again I wonder if he's coming on to me. His voice is lower by several octaves and his gaze never leaves my face.

I try for light and playful. "Thank you for your trust."

Carlo reaches across the table and with the flick of one finger touches my wrist at the pulse. "It's more than trust. Surely you must know that by now."

My fantasy has become reality. I am sitting here unable to speak. I bury my nose in the menu. I have dreamed about this moment for a long time.

"Have you made up your mind?" I ask, daring to look at him.

He sets the menu aside and looks me directly in the eye.

"I have."

"I'm having the escargot for an appetizer but I'm torn between the salmon and the fettuccine with shrimp and scallops."

"Get them both."

"I can't do that."

"Why not?"

Good point. I sip my wine and wonder why not. I've always been a good girl and I've always played by the rules. Not tonight. Tonight I am going to live out my fantasy. I am going to put Reed Samuels behind me and concentrate on this man who has fascinated me from the first moment I met him.

When the waiter comes over, Carlo flashes me his brilliant white smile and places our order. He's having the Chilean sea bass. Then he reaches across the table and threads his fingers through mine.

"I am captivated by you, bella," he says in the same tone as if he were asking me to pass the bread basket.

I swallow a mouthful of wine so fast I almost choke and wait for the liquid to settle.

He hands me his napkin.

"You are what they call the full package—hard working, self-sufficient, articulate and dangerously attractive. I cannot believe someone has not scooped you up."

Carlo's thumb makes circles on my hand. I am going to melt into the floor. I get hold of myself and ask the million-dollar question. "You are also single I presume?"

His smile is slow and easy. "Yes, I have been unattached for almost four years." He senses I am about to say something, so he holds up a finger. "So you understand I am by no means a monk. I date here and there but nothing serious."

The waiter returns with my appetizer and Carlo's

salad. While we eat, I replay our conversation in my head. It is quite obviously leading up to something.

When the entrées arrive—the two I have picked, plus his—he watches with amusement as I dive in.

"Dessert?" Carlo asks when we are through.

"Not for me." I am stuffed.

A gesture of one finger and the check arrives on a silver tray. A platinum card is handed over and quickly returned. Carlo stands and holds out his hand. I take it and follow him into an inner room where a jazz quartet plays the blues. I am swept up against his hard body and we begin to foxtrot. He is a good dancer, smooth as they come and easy to follow.

Carlo smells a bit like saffron and his body heat makes me heady, so heady I almost stumble over my feet. It gives him the excuse to pull me even closer. We sway in place, my head resting on his shoulder. When the song stops we continue to dance in slow motion. I can feel every taut inch of him.

Time passes. I am not sure how long. Finally the band stops playing and Carlo leads me off the floor.

"Shall we call it an evening, then?" he says.

I don't want it to end. I don't want to go home.

We head out to the valet to retrieve our respective cars. Dang but my cell phone chooses that moment to ring. I glance at the incoming number and grimace. Margot can't have picked a worse time to call.

"Do you have to get that?" Carlo asks when I make no effort to answer.

I hesitate but it is late and this may be a real emergency. I pick up. "What's up, Margot?"

"I can't talk long. Earl's coming over. I just wanted to let you know Reed responded to the fictitious profile we posted. He's quite the player. He's looking to set up a date."

I feel a sharp stab of pain. Again I feel betrayed. "You can't let that happen."

She laughs raucously. "Already done."

I struggle to breathe.

"He'll get stood up," Margot says, and cackles again.

I sense Carlo tuned in and listening.

"I have to go." I slip my cell phone back into my purse.

"Is everything okay, Roxanne?"

"Couldn't be better."

I've gotten closure at last. This whole sordid situation has nothing to do with me. It's all about Reed Samuels, a very confused man.

The valets are waiting with our cars.

Carlo walks me to the Land Rover. He tugs on my hand. "I wish you would come home with me."

I smile up at him. "I thought you'd never ask."

Carlo DeAngelo is more of a man than Reed Samuels ever could hope to be. He doesn't play mind games, and that in and of itself says something.

Featuring the voices of eighteen of your
favorite authors…

ON THE LINE

Essence Bestselling Author
donna hill

A sexy, irresistible story starring Joy Newhouse,
who, as a radio relationship expert, is considered
the diva of the airwaves. But when she's fired,
Joy quickly discovers that if she can dish it out,
she'd better be able to take it!

Featuring contributions by such favorite authors
as Gwynne Forster, Monica Jackson, Earl Sewell,
Phillip Thomas Duck and more!

Coming the first week of January,
wherever books are sold.

sepia™

www.kimanipress.com

KPDH0211207TR

Because even the smartest women can make
relationship mistakes...

ACCLAIMED AUTHOR
JEWEL DIAMOND TAYLOR

A straight-to-the point book that will empower women
and help them overcome such self-defeating emotions as
insecurity, desperation, jealousy, loneliness...all factors that
can keep you in a destructive cycle of unloving, unfulfilling
relationships. Through the powerful insights and life-lessons
in this book, you will learn to build a relationship that's
strong enough to last a lifetime.

"Jewel Diamond Taylor captivates audiences. She moves the spirit."
—Susan L. Taylor, Editorial Director, *Essence* magazine

Available the first week of January, wherever books are sold.

tangled
ROOTS

A Kendra Clayton Novel

ANGELA
HENRY

Nothing's going right these days for part-time
English teacher and reluctant sleuth Kendra Clayton.
Now her favorite student is the number one suspect in a local
murder. When he begs Kendra for help, she's soon on the road
to trouble again—trying to find the real killer, stepping into
danger...and getting tangled in the deadly roots of desire.

"This debut mystery features an exciting new
African-American heroine.... Highly recommended."
—*Library Journal* on *The Company You Keep*

**Available the first week of May
wherever books are sold.**

KIMANI PRESS™
www.kimanipress.com

KPAH0680507TR

A brand-new Kendra Clayton mystery
from acclaimed author…

ANGELA HENRY

Diva's Last Curtain Call

Amateur sleuth Kendra Clayton finds herself immersed in
mayhem once again when a cunning killer rolls credits on a
fading movie star. Kendra's publicity-seeking sister is pegged
as the prime suspect, but Kendra knows her sister is no
murderer. She soon uncovers some surprising Hollywood
secrets, putting herself in danger of becoming the killer's
encore performance....

"A tightly woven mystery."
—*Ebony* magazine on *The Company You Keep*

sepia™

*Coming the first
week of June
wherever books
are sold.*

A volume of heartwarming devotionals
that will nourish your soul...

NORMA DeSHIELDS BROWN

Joy

COMES THIS MORNING

Norma DeShields Brown's life suddenly changed
when her only son was tragically taken from her
by a senseless act. Consumed by grief, she began
an intimate journey that became
Joy Comes This Morning.

Filled with thoughtful devotions, Scripture readings
and words of encouragement, this powerful book
will guide you on a spiritual journey that will sustain
you throughout the years.

*Available the first week of November
wherever books are sold.*

NEW SPIRIT
TM

www.kimanipress.com

KPNDB0351107TR

GET THE GENUINE LOVE
YOU DESERVE...

NATIONAL BESTSELLING AUTHOR

Vikki Johnson

Addicted to COUNTERFEIT LOVE

Many people in today's world are unable to recognize
what a genuine loving partnership should be and
often sabotage one when it does come along. In this
moving volume, Vikki Johnson offers memorable
words that will help readers identify destructive love
patterns and encourage them to demand the love
that they are entitled to.

Available the first week of October wherever books are sold.

A soul-stirring, compelling
journey of self-discovery…

*j*ourney
into My Brother's Soul

Maria D. Dowd

Bestselling author of
Journey to Empowerment

A memorable collection of essays, prose and poetry,
reflecting the varied experiences that men of color face
throughout life. Touching on every facet of living—love,
marriage, fatherhood, family—these candid personal
contributions explore the essence of what it means to
be a man today.

**"*Journey to Empowerment* will lead you on a
healing journey and will lead to a great love of self,
and a deeper understanding of the many roles we
all must play in life."—*Rawsistaz Reviewers***

Coming the first week of May
wherever books are sold.

www.kimanipress.com   KPMDD0290507TR